Strike Out

Roz Lee

DEDICATION

To my readers.

You make the work worthwhile.

.

ACKNOWLEDGMENTS

I really must thank my family for all their support. They've stood behind me from the beginning, and I can't tell you how much that means to me.

I also want to thank the wonderful people who buy and read my books. Without readers there would be no writers. I'm blessed to have the best readers in the world.

CHAPTER ONE

Royce gazed down at the sparkling emerald and rust diamond he considered home. Devoid of players at this hour, the smell of sweet-mown grass and the silence of thousands of empty seats called to him. He closed his eyes, imagining lying in the center of the outfield, arms outstretched, and the peace he would find there. Inhaling deep, he held the stale, chilled office air in his lungs for a moment before exhaling.

Turning to the Mustangs' manager, he asked, "Why me?"

Doyle Walker raised one eyebrow. "Why not you?"

"Everyone else said no, right?"

"They all have their reasons, but trumped-up excuses aside, you make the most sense. I have no idea if this technology has any value or not, but if there is any possibility it can help you regain ground, then we have to give it a try."

"You mean *I* have to give it a try."

The older man acknowledged the truth in Royce's statement with a slight nod. "Yes, *you* have to give it a try. Conventional means aren't working for you, and since I can't make you see a shrink, this is my next best option."

He didn't need a shrink to tell him his lack-luster performance on the field was all in his head. Other players had played through divorce without a ripple in their career. But not him. Intellectually, he understood his marriage had been over for a long time before Hannah asked for a divorce, but still, the hurt in her eyes, in her voice, when she uttered those words had turned him inside out.

Failure was new to him. Always the golden boy, he'd succeeded at everything he'd ever tried—except making Hannah happy. Since he first laid eyes on her in junior high school, all he'd wanted to do was make her smile. Knowing he'd failed at such an important task had changed him. He'd lost his mojo. He was off his game, physically.

He gave his all on the field, but suddenly, his all sucked. Doyle was right. He had to do something, or his career would be over sooner rather than later.

Returning his gaze to the field some five stories below, he knew he had no choice. He was going to become a guinea pig in the name of science.

"When?"

"Dr. Reed will be here this afternoon. Two o'clock. Martin's old office."

"How long?"

"We agreed on a month with the stipulation you would be available the entire time, however many hours it takes."

He felt the heavy weight of obligation on his shoulders, turning his blood to slow-moving sludge. "A whole freakin' month?"

"You've got something else to do?" Doyle's statement was laden with sarcasm. Royce's time belonged to the Mustangs, and they both knew it.

"No. A month just sounds like a long time to spend on one research subject." Like he knew jack-shit about scientific research.

"If things go well, Dr. Reed may add players. But the first two weeks, at least, it's only you."

"Great." He could do sarcasm, too. With one last look at

the field, Royce turned his back on the expansive plate-glass window. His gaze swept the office. He'd never wanted a regular job, one that included a desk in an office, but as offices went, Doyle's was the best he'd ever seen. Years of memorabilia from his playing years, along with awards and photos from his stint as the Mustangs' manager lined the walls. Royce admired the wide bookcase to the right of the manager's desk. He imagined how it would look in the library of his new house. Mentally noting to search for something similar, he crossed the room for a closer look.

"Don't you want to know about the research?"

"Nope." The edict had come down from the mountain, and there wasn't a thing he could do to change it. "What's with the bat?" He'd noticed it before but never had the opportunity to examine it. On a stand, encased in glass, it was unmistakably old. He edged closer, trying to make out the signature on the barrel.

"It was my granddad's." Doyle joined him in front of the artifact. "He used it during the 1936 season."

He felt like an idiot. Why hadn't he put two and two together before? "Your grandfather was Jimmy Doyle Walker? I thought you were just named after him or something."

"I *was* named after him. I've always gone by Doyle though."

"He was a great player."

"He was." Hearing the reverence in his voice, Royce turned to see him gazing at the keepsake. "I keep it here to remind me that everyone deserves a second chance. Even you."

He swallowed hard. "I appreciate it. I really do."

Doyle clapped him on the back. "Look, Royce. There's another reason I chose you to head up this research project." With a sweep of his hand, the manager indicated a casual grouping of chairs across the room. Royce took a seat and waited for the other shoe to fall.

"I want you to be my ears and eyes on this project. It sounds good on the surface, but in the wrong hands…." He shook his head. "I've been in this game my entire life. I know everything there is to know about baseball, and one thing I'm absolutely sure of is the most important factor in winning and losing is the human factor. No amount of empirical data can account for what's going on in a person's head."

Doyle leaned forward, bracing his forearms on his knees, his hands clasp together in front of him. "The game is dynamic, changing with the times. We've got instant replay now. Cameras everywhere, recording every possible angle. Economists analyzing players, valuing them based on individual plays instead of the person as a whole and what he brings to the team. You can't quantify team spirit, and sometimes heart is more valuable than the ability to hit consistently or strike batters out."

Royce's heart thudded. "I'll get back in the game. I promise."

Doyle sat up, relaxed. "I know you will. You love the game, and it shows. Whatever is wrong, you'll fix it. I've never had any doubt about that, son. As I said, if there's any merit in this research, then take advantage of it. But I need you to do something for me."

"Anything." He meant it. Everyone on the team knew how lucky they were to play for Doyle Walker, him included. He'd do whatever the man asked.

"Keep a close watch on this research project. Find out everything you can about the kind of data being collected and how this Dr. Reed plans to use it. The order to participate in this project came down from the League offices. I couldn't say no, but my acceptance doesn't mean I'm one hundred percent onboard with it. Maybe I'm old school, but I don't think everything has to be computer analyzed. Some things should be left alone."

Royce stalked down the hall to the training room. He'd spent the last four hours dreading his participation in this experiment, but Doyle was right, there was more to it than fixing his pitching—though he was at the point he'd try just about anything. He owed it to the team to give this a try. Hell, he owed it to Hannah, too. All his ex-wife had ever wanted for him was to be a success at the one thing he loved—baseball. She'd stuck by him through college and the lean years in the Minor League, offering encouragement and support when he'd needed it the most.

The irony of his present situation wasn't lost on him. Without Hannah's support, he might not have realized his dream of making it to the Major League, and now, here he was with his career on the line because he'd fucked up the single most important relationship of his life. He hadn't been there when his wife needed him. She'd given him everything, and in return, he'd given her nothing.

She had gone back to school to get her degree—something he'd insisted on paying for above and beyond everything she'd asked for in the divorce settlement. It was the least he could do since she'd dropped out of school to follow him around the country from one Minor League hovel to another. At the time, she'd said it was what she wanted to do, and he'd been selfish enough to believe her.

Years passed, and it never once crossed his mind she might not be happy with her decision. Either she was an expert at hiding her unhappiness, or he had been too wrapped up in his career to notice.

She'd said the same thing—only, she'd been kinder, saying they'd grown apart, which was code for he'd fucked up.

With nothing else to fill his life besides his career now, he was in serious danger of fucking that up, too.

There wasn't a damn thing wrong with him physically, but if this experiment forced him to think about something besides what he'd lost, then maybe there was a chance he could salvage what was left of his life. He loved baseball.

It was his love of the game that kept him moving down the hallway toward the training room on his day off. Entering the large room filled with physical therapy equipment, he nodded to a couple of players on the Disabled list who were there pushing through the pain of recovery under the watchful eyes of staff. He noted the curiosity on their faces but figured word would spread fast enough on its own and kept on walking.

The office assigned to Dr. Reed was on the right, halfway down. Peeking through the narrow safety-glass window above the door handle, he paused. He might be in mourning for his marriage, but he wasn't dead. His heart rate kicked up and blood rushed south.

Standing in front of the desk, her back to him, was the shapeliest pixy he'd ever seen. No more than five foot three in her white canvas sneakers, she looked like a teenager, which meant she was a summer intern, and thus—off-limits. Didn't mean he couldn't look, and admire.

Blonde hair streaked with gold tumbled down her slender back to just below her shoulder blades. The Mustangs' red cotton shirt she wore hugged her waist before flaring out over generous hips clad in white shorts that emphasized her tanned legs. Cheerleader material, he determined. A staff member's daughter or niece working for free so they'd have something to put on their college applications this year—or maybe next.

At twenty-six, as far as he was concerned teenagers were nothing more than jailbait, but they couldn't arrest him for looking.

Pulling the door open, he stepped inside. Completely absorbed in what she was doing, she didn't seem to notice she was no longer alone. She muttered something sounding like a very un-pixy-like curse. Royce smiled. He could relate to her frustration.

"Need some help?" He rounded the desk to see what had her so worked up and stopped dead in his tracks. If she was older than eighteen, he'd eat his cleats, dirt and all. And, Lord, even with a scowl on her face, she was a beautiful creature.

Determination flashed in her eyes, and though her lips were turned down, they were full and naturally rose-colored. Unless she was a magician with cosmetics, she didn't wear a stitch of makeup. You couldn't improve on perfection, no use trying.

Whoever brought her to work here ought to be shot. The older players would look but keep their hands to themselves. The younger ones, not so much. They'd recently brought a relief pitcher up from the Minors who was barely legal to drink, which made him three bricks shy of a full load of self-control. The idiot had a different woman on his arm every time Royce saw him. He'd be damned if he let the hurler get his hands on this sweet, innocent thing.

As a protectiveness he'd never experienced before flooded his system, the object of his unusual possessiveness returned her attention to her task, leaving him to reach his own conclusion.

Royce grabbed a clump of wires and began to work the knots out. She wound another loose wire around her fingers before setting the neat coil aside. "I can do this myself."

"No problem. I'm supposed to meet someone here at two. I don't suppose you know if a Dr. Reed has arrived, do you?"

The girl stilled, her gaze lifting to his face. "Why?"

"I'm not sick or anything, if that's what you're worried about. Dr. Reed is doing research on…." He scrunched his eyebrows together, thinking. "Hell, I don't know. Something to do with how athletes move."

"What does her project have to do with you?"

Her gaze had somehow gone from mild interest to intense assessment. A shimmer of unease traveled along his spine. He felt as if he'd tripped an invisible cord that, with his next breath, would blow his world to smithereens. "I'm the designated guinea pig."

"You're Royce Stryker?"

"Who are you?"

They voiced their questions simultaneously.

"I asked you first." He dumped his handful of wires to the desk then took a step back.

"No, you didn't, but I'll answer anyway." She squared her shoulders, making her look every bit of five foot three and a half. "I'm Doctor Reed. Tricia Reed. Not Patricia, just Tricia."

"Is this some sort of a joke?" He reclaimed the distance between himself and the desk, squaring his shoulders, too, employing every inch of his six-foot frame to let her know how not funny this was. "Who are you, really? Who put you up to this?"

Not waiting for her reply, he barreled on. "I can't believe anyone in this organization would be stupid enough to turn a little girl like you loose in a place like this. You're somebody's kid or niece or something. Who? Tell me, and I'll knock sense into them instead of paddling your ass."

An entirely inappropriate image of her bent over the desk, those shorts around her ankles, his handprints on her sweet cheeks, formed in his mind, nearly blinding him with lust. With supreme effort, he forced the scene to recede. Focusing on the girl across from him, he couldn't believe his eyes. She smiled at him. Smiled! She had moxie, he'd give her that.

"What's so funny?"

"You. You think you can spank me?"

"I know I can." What was he saying? He'd never spanked a girl before, and he'd damn sure lose his job if he touched this one. She belonged to someone—someone important in the organization—or she wouldn't be interning here.

"No, you think you can. Trust me, if you try, you won't like the outcome. Not only do I have advanced degrees in Sports Medicine, Anatomy, and Neuro-Biology, but I have a black belt in Tae Kwon Do, too." She had the nerve to smirk at him. "Still think you can spank me, Royce?"

Royce. His name on her lips stunned him. *Royce. Royce. Royce.* When she said it, it sounded like an invitation or maybe a challenge. He didn't give a good goddamn which. He wanted to hear her say it again, preferably while she was lying across his lap, accepting punishment for…. He shook his head to clear the rapidly degenerating images.

He nodded. "Oh, yeah. But I want to hear you beg me, first." He didn't know what had come over him to be goading her like this. She couldn't be who she said she was. He let his gaze roam over her body again, stopping at her breasts. They were small, perhaps because she was still a child.

"Eyes," she said, "up here." She gestured with two fingers for him look up. He forced his gaze to move north. "I don't know what kind of women you've been dating if you expect me to beg you to do anything."

It didn't take much imagination to see her beneath him, begging, but he kept the thought to himself. "I don't date."

Her eyebrows rose at his harsh response. "You don't date, Royce?"

There it was it was again, his name spoken as if she were daring him to come and kiss it off her lips. He opened his mouth to correct her, but she didn't give him time to respond to her provocative statement.

"Since you don't date, then I will assume you're married. Okay. Fair enough." She waved his marital status away. "Doesn't matter to me."

The more she talked, the more his body betrayed him. He hated that he wanted her more than he could remember ever wanting a woman before, even Hannah. Even though the divorce had been final for nearly a year, wanting another woman felt like a betrayal and tasted bitter in his mouth. The one thing that hadn't been messed up in their marriage was their sex life. He might have neglected her other needs, but physically, she'd been satisfied. But, as she had pointed out to him with a wide expanse of a conference room desk between them, sex wasn't enough.

"How old are you? Twelve?" He instantly regretted his words. All playfulness in Dr. Reed disappeared faster than beer at an Octoberfest. She narrowed her eyes so her gaze became an uncomfortable laser aimed straight at him.

"I'm twenty-five. Old enough that I don't have to put up with any kind of shit from you or anyone else."

She'd defended herself plenty, he could tell.

"I graduated from high school when I was fourteen. I got my first bachelor's degree when I was sixteen and my first PhD when I was twenty. I have six advanced degrees, and did I mention the black belt?"

"You mentioned it."

"What about you, Einstein?"

"Stryker. The name is Stryker. I have a bachelor's degree in Marketing."

"Then you can read and write. Good. I was worried about I might be working with illiterates." She reached for a worn canvas briefcase on the corner of the desk, drew out a sheaf of papers then held them out to him. "Fill these out. Don't skip any lines. If you don't know how to answer, ask me. I need all the information to establish a base line for you."

Torn between apologizing for asking a simple question and responding to her last insult, he took the papers from her. She was worried he wouldn't be able to read and write? What the fuck? Almost every player he knew at least had a bachelor's degree. And most of the ones who didn't were young and still working on theirs. Everyone needed something to fall back on in case of injury or if they simply couldn't cut it any longer against the new players coming up.

He looked around for a pen, found one in a coffee cup turned desk accessory, then sat in the desk chair. Dr. Reed, age twenty-five, dragged a pile of wires out of the way so he'd have a place to write.

"What are all those?"

"Electrodes and sensors."

CHAPTER TWO

The blood drained from her subject's face leaving him pale and visibly shaking. If Tricia hadn't been so pissed, she might have found the situation funny. Who knew a healthy male could pale so quickly? And, God, was he healthy. Why couldn't they have sent her a guy with a pot-belly and stained teeth? Royce Stryker was six-foot-something of pure perfection. If she'd had one of those build-a-body books where you flip pages, choosing face, torso, and legs to put together your ideal man, she would have ended up with Royce. Dark hair, lean face with eyes the color of a deep, pure lake. Straight, even teeth and lips that would probably send her into a swoon if they ever smiled.

She couldn't let him see her attraction. Like a physician, she needed to keep a professional distance from the people she worked with. Doing so would have been so much easier with a tobacco-chewing, beer-drinking slob.

"You have a problem with wearing sensors?"

He shook his head, but the color of his skin said otherwise.

Great. Just great. The last thing she wanted to do was babysit a grown man with phobias. "Look." She picked one of the tiny electrodes up to show him. "It's like a Band-Aid. Peel and stick. Nothing punctures the skin, I promise."

"No needles?"

He was talking again. Color was returning to his cheeks, but his eyes were still glassy and distant. Not good. "No needles, though I would like to get a blood test before we begin. It's part of establishing the base line I talked about. You know, in case there are factors that could influence the results of the experiment."

At the mention of the blood work, his skin paled again. *Of all the players in the Major League, I got the only squeamish one. Just my luck.* Nothing about this project had been easy thus far, so she had no reason to expect this part to be any different, yet, she had hoped. It had taken nearly a year of meetings to convince the national organization her research could be valuable, and almost as long to reach an agreement with the Mustangs' management to allow her to use a sampling of their players as subjects. Now this. Her first subject was a wimp.

"You've had blood tests before, right?"

He nodded.

"And you survived them or you wouldn't be here now."

Another nod.

"Then you'll survive one more."

His head swiveled from side to side.

Tricia blew out a breath. "When was your last physical?"

"Spring Training. March."

Four months. Unacceptable if she wanted her results to mean anything. She shook her head. "Nope. Won't do. I need more current data, or any conclusions I reach will be subject to question. I need a clean base line."

"I didn't agree to be poked with needles."

His color was returning along with his spirit. This she could deal with. "Look. Why don't you fill out the paperwork first? The team doctor agreed to draw the...." He was turning pale again. She changed tactics. "He said he would do the test."

She picked up the pen he'd dropped and held it up, inviting him to take it. "I'll hold your hand through the whole thing. I promise." She'd do anything, including babysit a grown man to get this project underway.

He lifted his chin, and Tricia found her gaze captured by his. No longer glassy, his eyes smoldered with determination and resolve. She might have jerked the rug from under his feet with the whole blood-test thing, but he'd undoubtedly found the inner strength to overcome his fear. Damn. That was sexy.

"I don't need you to hold my hand." Said appendage closed around hers, and for the span of a heartbeat, Tricia felt lightheaded. Searing heat liquefied every muscle in her body and vaporized the air in her lungs. She gasped and jerked away from his touch.

"O-okay." She schooled her expression to the professional façade she'd worked hard to cultivate. "Today. You'll do it today?"

"As soon as I finish this mountain of paperwork."

Tricia took solace in his brusque tone, an indication he had recovered his equilibrium. She only wished she could say the same herself. She could still feel the imprint of his palm over the back of her hand, could still feel the lingering warmth low in her body. It was nothing more than a primal response— as old as mankind, but new to her.

She untangled another wire while silently thanking the thoughtless assistant who had tossed the expensive equipment into the case without taking the time to properly store it. While carefully working another snarl loose, she studied the man sitting at the desk. Whatever she'd felt when he touched her must have been one-sided. He'd reacted strongly to the mention of a blood test, but touching her? Nothing. Nada. Not even a flicker of awareness on his part for something that had sent her heart rate into the stratosphere.

Tiny tingling sensations still danced on her skin. Yet, he continued to mark down answers as if nothing had happened.

A trained observer, she noted the return of his normal coloring. Though tanned from hours in the sun, his natural coloring, judging from the band of skin she'd glimpsed below his collar when he bent forward, looked to be a light shade of gold. She'd know for certain soon enough. In order to collect all the data needed, she would have to attach sensors to almost every part of his body.

He wouldn't be the first man she'd wired, but none of the others had elicited any sort of physical response from her through casual physical contact. A few had tried out their wittiest pickup lines while she attached sensors to various parts of their anatomy, but they'd laughed with her when she rolled her eyes and tugged to make sure the adhesive held.

Concentrating on a pesky knot, she let her mind wander further afield. If merely touching his hand had elicited such a primal response in her, what would happen when she touched his biceps? Or his pectorals? Or his abdominals? Would she feel the same overwhelming feeling, or would it be business as usual?

"Why do you need to know this?" Royce's baritone snapped her out of her thoughts.

"Hmm?"

"Number forty. How many times do you have sex in a week? What does my sex life have to do with anything?"

"Sexual activity can be a marker for overall health."

He tapped the clicker end of his pen on the form in a jittery rhythm while he reread the question, presumably considering it in a different light, thanks to her explanation. Tricia resumed her task, hoping and praying he'd write something down and move on to the next question. She didn't want to think about him having sex. After her reaction earlier, imagining him having sex with her wasn't much of a stretch, and that was the *last* thing she needed to be thinking about.

"Does masturbation count? Or only sex with a partner?"

Tricia's fingers tightened on the thin wires in her hand. *He didn't really just ask about solo sex, did he?* Her ears had to be playing tricks on her. "What?"

"Does masturbation count as sex? That's all I want to know."

"Uh. I...." *Does it?* Why hadn't she thought of it before? Why hadn't any of the other men who'd answered the questions asked? "No." She closed her eyes. "Yes. I don't know."

When she opened her eyes, Royce Stryker was looking at her, a giant smile transforming his already handsome face into a work of art. The same heated rush she'd experienced when he touched her consumed her once again. The cartilage in her knees softened. She placed her hands flat on the desk for support.

His embarrassment at the prospect of writing a big, fat zero in the space provided, unless masturbation counted, was nothing compared to the entertainment value of watching Dr. Tricia Reed grapple with his question. Since his wife left him, his only sexual companion had been his right hand. For most of those months, he'd admit, the woman on his mind had been Hannah, but as time moved on, so had his imagination. More and more, the female on his mind was someone he'd recently met, or the occasional actress in the news. No doubt, tonight a certain scientist with big eyes, small breasts, and tanned legs would star in his private musings.

The author of the infernal questionnaire hunched forward, using her hands to support herself over the desk, giving Royce a perfect view down the front of her V-neck shirt. He almost swallowed his tongue. *Jesus.* Her breasts weren't small. They were perfect. His palms itched to feel their weight, to lift them to his lips.

He shifted, trying to relieve the pressure in his jeans. Not even the threat of a blood test could make him not want her. Hell, she could make a dead man rise. And wasn't that what he'd been for the last few months? Dead? *Not anymore.*

"Well? How should I answer the question?"

"Maybe you could average the two over the last year?"

"Okay." He wrote a number in the blank space. "Seven it is."

"You have sex seven times a week?"

Royce smiled at the disbelief in her voice.

"No. I masturbate seven times a week. On average." And, he knew without a doubt, the number was going to increase, now that he'd met Dr. Reed. His mind was already coming up with fantasy scenarios to accompany the hand action. "Do you have a lab coat?"

"What? Why?"

I'll take that as a yes. Royce smiled. "Nothing." He turned his attention to the next question, which, thankfully, asked about his eating habits.

The team's medical staff, having dealt with him before, understood his limitations when it came to needles and blood. The nurse practitioner, Mary Alice something-or-other, let him lie on the exam table during the procedure, so if he passed out, he wouldn't end up on the floor. While she searched his arm for a suitable place to drain his life force, he turned his head and closed his eyes. Immediately, his mind conjured fantasies of the fabulous Dr. Tricia Reed draining him in a much more pleasant way.

He saw black the instant the needle pricked his skin, coming to when Mary Alice patted his cheek with her latex-clad fingers.

"All done?" He tried to sit up, but a firm hand on his shoulder was all it took to keep him on his back.

"All done. Just lie there for a few minutes." She shook her head. "I've never seen anyone as weak as you when it comes to blood work. Boggles the mind."

Royce blanched at the sound of her removing her gloves. He hated that sound.

"Let me get you something to drink." For a woman in her mid-fifties, she had a nice ass. As she walked away, he pushed to a sitting position. The room spun once or twice, but by the time she returned with a glass of orange juice, he was feeling better.

"Thanks." He took a sip. "Let's not do this again anytime soon."

"Hey. Wasn't my idea this time. But you know how I enjoy seeing you suffer…."

"Wasn't my idea either."

"Who's Tricia?"

The name hit him like a sucker punch. "Huh?"

"Don't play stupid with me. You always talk when you're out of it. Used to be you talked about Hannah, but today it was Tricia."

Royce frowned. Why didn't he know this about himself? He resolved then and there to avoid blood work for the rest of his life. "Nobody."

He mentally patted himself on the back for pulling the lie off with such ease. Tricia Reed, in the span of an hour, had wormed her way into his life and, apparently, his subconscious, too. But she wasn't going any further. He'd done the relationship thing, had the divorce papers to prove it. Not to mention, he was supposed to be keeping an eye on her research.

"She wouldn't be the researcher I heard about, would she?"

"Mind your own business." The words were meant as a warning, but his delivery insured Mary Alice wouldn't take offense.

"You are my business, Stryker. I love you guys. Why else would I hang around this place?"

He slid off the table. Finding his feet steady beneath him, he headed for the door, calling over his shoulder as he went, "You know you stay because of the hot bodies you get to touch. Don't think we don't know it, too!"

A rather unladylike word followed him from the room. He might not like what she did, but he loved Mary Alice like a mother. They all did.

Tricia thumbed through the questionnaire, checking to make sure Mustangs Test Subject #1, MTS1, for short, had answered every question. The second time around, she glanced at the answers to confirm his understanding of the question and appropriateness of the answer. With previous subjects, she'd never had a single qualm about reading their responses to the highly personal questions, but somehow, reading Royce's neatly penned answers made her feel like a Peeping Tom.

By the time she reached the end of the document, she knew more about him than he probably knew about himself. She'd bet he didn't know his weekly alcohol consumption was well below the average for men his age or his usual six hours of sleep nightly could be a contributing factor to his on-field problems. She'd have to talk to him about those issues. In order for her data to be meaningful, he'd need to be well rested.

Which brought her to question number forty. He'd checked divorced under marital status on the first page, which made his inquiry regarding masturbation a bit more understandable. She stared at the number scrawled in the box. Seven. On average.

She vaguely recalled reading somewhere that men were prone to exaggeration when it came to their sex lives, but why would any man admit to masturbation being his sole sexual outlet, much less report taking matters into his own hand seven times a week? *On average.*

He hadn't sounded as if he were bragging. No, he'd simply been stating a fact. One she couldn't credit. Divorced or not, the man was beyond hot. He was also wealthy and a professional athlete. If he wanted sexual partners, he could have them.

Which meant he didn't want them.

Was he still in love with his ex-wife? That would explain his solo sex for the last year or so. She made a note to herself to find out when he'd gotten divorced. The information didn't matter to her research, but the idea of a virile man like Royce Stryker not pursuing natural inclinations was troubling. As a scientist, it was her job to explore every possible factor that could influence the results of her experiment.

She scribbled another note in her lab book. *Does masturbation = sex w/ partner? Does lack of sexual partners = decreased libido? Check testosterone levels on MTS1.*

Under Observations, she wrote – *Casual observation does not indicate a lower than normal testosterone level. In fact, MTS1 exhibits physical attributes consistent with high levels of T hormone. i.e. pronounced Adam's Apple, deep voice, pronounced facial hair mid-afternoon. NOTE: Could be from lack of personal grooming in morning. Requires further observation.*

Tricia flipped the notebook closed. *Or I could just ask him.* Another first. She'd never felt compelled to ask any of her college-aged subjects if they'd shaved or not. A few of them had exhibited five o'clock shadows early in the day, but most of them probably could have skipped a day shaving and no one would have noticed. She doubted that was the case with Royce Stryker. She'd bet her next pedicure the man shaved twice a day.

She was still contemplating what his T levels could mean in terms of her research when MTS1 returned from his blood test. He walked with a confident gate, no sign of the distress he'd exhibited when he left for the innocuous procedure. Either he was supremely pleased with himself for surviving or he'd been somewhere else for the last half hour. Tricia narrowed her eyes at him.

"What?" he asked, stopping in front of her desk.

"Where have you been?"

"I went to see Mary Alice." He stretched his arm out, revealing a cartoon bandage holding a cotton ball in place. "All done."

"And you lived to tell about it. Amazing."

"Hey, do not underestimate medical procedures. They can be dangerous."

She couldn't help it, she rolled her eyes. "No one has ever died from a blood test."

"Can I see that in writing?"

She stood, reaching for the bag where she'd stored all the sensors she'd spent a good part of the day untangling. "No, you can't. But you can take your clothes off."

He froze, his eyes wide, cheeks flushed with color. "What?"

Assuming a stance she hoped conveyed a no-nonsense professional demeanor, she stared him down. "Should I have your hearing tested, too? I said, take your clothes off. You can leave your underwear on. It won't be in the way."

Expecting him to comply, she turned her back to him to dig in her bag for the box of self-adhesive electrode pads she'd brought. As she dug to the bottom, the rustling of cloth told her MTS1 was doing as she'd asked. Nakedness had never been an issue with previous test subjects, but the idea of this one disrobing in her presence did crazy things to her body. She forced her lungs to take deep, measured breaths, and though she'd easily located the small box, she continued to feel around in the bag, willing her out-of-control heart rate to go back to normal.

This is so not good. Get a grip, Dr. Reed. Be professional. He's just a test subject—nothing more.

She'd just about convinced herself the man behind her was just like all the other men she'd tested in her research—then she turned around.

Holy bejesus!

Tricia reached for the desk behind her. Tossing the box of electrodes on the surface, she gripped the edge with both hands to keep from melting into a puddle of lust. MTS1 was definitely not one of the college subjects she'd tested. Holy crap, they were mere boys compared to the specimen standing before her wearing nothing but socks and the briefest briefs she'd ever seen. Shit. Her panties contained more cloth, or maybe it just seemed that way because his tented outward to cover....

Oh, Lord.

"See anything you like?"

Tricia snapped her gaze away from Royce's impressive

groin so fast her vision clouded. When she focused again, he was grinning at her as if to say, "I know, I'm perfect. Look all you want." His arrogance was all she needed to remind her who she was and why she was there.

"No," she said, forcing her gaze to travel down his magnificent chest, skipping the navy-blue cotton briefs to take in his thick thighs and muscular calves. Stifling a giggle at the hole in the toe of one of his socks, she returned her gaze to his. "On second thought, we can't do this right now."

"Why not?" He actually sounded peeved she wasn't going to wire him up today then put him through his paces, though she conceded, he didn't really have any idea what awaited him. He'd know soon enough.

She risked sliding to the floor by releasing her grip on the desk to wave a hand at his admittedly perfect body. "You'll have to shave first."

He rubbed his jaw, his eyes reflecting his confusion. "I shaved this morning."

Scratch checking T levels. No problem there. "I mean, you'll have to shave…or wax…." She waved her hand up and down. "All of it. Chest. Legs. Arms."

"You're fuckin' kidding me!" His biceps flexed as he placed his fisted hands on his hips.

She'd never told a subject to shave before, but then again, she'd never had one with so much body hair. Christ. He wasn't a bear or anything, but jeez, if she attached the pads to him, they would be hell to get off. "I'm not kidding." Finding her equilibrium in her superior knowledge on this subject, she reached for the box she'd dropped. Opening it, she pulled out an individually wrapped package, tore it open, and held the object up for his inspection. "These are like adhesive bandages."

She pulled off the paper backing, showing him the sticky side of the pad. "I can put these on you, but you won't like it when they come off. It'll hurt like hell."

His eyes widened as realization dawned on him. Pleased he'd, at last, come to his senses and would voluntarily do some hair removal, she was surprised when he just stood there.

"Well?" she asked.

"Well, what?"

"Aren't you going to go shave?"

"No."

"Why the hell not?"

He looked taken aback by the shrillness in her voice, and truth be told, it concerned her, too. But god or not, the man's lack of cooperation was getting to her. Nevertheless, she needed him, so she cleared her throat and tried again. "Sorry. What I meant to say was, I don't want to hurt you. Body hair won't affect my research, as long as the pads adhere tight enough, and I'm sure they will. My concern is for you."

She didn't think he could make himself look more stoic, but he did, squaring his shoulders and fixing her with a stern look that dared her to question his manhood again.

"I've worn bandages before." He didn't even flinch as he said it.

"Okay, then." She peeled the backing off the pad in her hand, and slapped it against his chest directly above his left nipple. The muscles were hard as rock beneath skin she found surprisingly warm. A smile formed in her mind, but she wouldn't let it show on her face. The skin beneath the pad she'd just applied, and the next one attached to his right pectoral, was very sensitive. He was going to cry like a baby when she pulled those off.

He stood still as a monument while she attached the rest of the pads. His macho, I-can-take-it attitude jabbed at something inside her, and when she had a choice between a lightly haired section of skin, like the top of his calf muscle just below the knee joint, or the center of the same muscle, she chose the latter. *We'll see how you like that, Mr. Macho Baseball Player.*

CHAPTER THREE

"Are you about done?" She'd stopped sticking things to his body, thank God, and moved on to attaching things to the sticky things. As she clamped a gizmo to a pad attached to his right thigh, he glanced down. Wires hung from his chest, arms, and abdomen. He looked like an abandoned building wired for demolition. But that wasn't what concerned him.

It was the woman on her knees in front of him. God, she was beautiful. Almost pixy-like in stature, but she was anything but fragile. He'd come up against her iron will a couple of times already, and shit, if seeing her mouth a few inches from his junk wasn't enough to make him beg, knowing the strength contained in her petite body was.

He forced his gaze up to the white board mounted on the wall behind the desk, and in an effort to distract his mind—and his cock—from the female at his feet, he focused on the trainer's schedule for the next week.

"What happens when we're out of town?"

"I'm going with you. On your days off, we'll do some basic stuff, like today. During games, I'll monitor you remotely so

I'll have two sets of data to compare. Workout mode and game mode."

"What do you mean, you'll monitor remotely? I can't pitch with all these wires hanging off me."

"You won't have to. You'll still have the pads, but the electrodes will be wireless." She stood and, going to her bag, produced a handful of microchips with tails attached.

"They look like alien sperm."

Her husky laugh was a cattle prod to his groin. His dick responded, ready for action. *Shit.* And he had nothing to hide behind.

She sorted one from the bunch before placing the rest back in the bag. When she turned to him, a single example rested on her palm. "They do sort of resemble sperm, don't they?" She flicked it with one perfect, but unpainted, fingernail. "These are a whole lot smarter than sperm, though. These can differentiate between a thousand different movements, whereas the real ones can only focus on one thing."

He knew he was going to hate himself for asking, but the words were out of his mouth before he could stop them. "And what is that?"

"Being first in line." She picked up the little guy by his tail, dangling him in the air while she examined it from all angles. "You see, it's in their genetics to be first. First to penetrate the woman, whether they admit it or not, first to penetrate the egg, first in line, first to fly, first in space, first to cross the finish line, first, first, first. It never ends."

"First to score."

She smiled, palming the device again. "Exactly." She placed her show-and-tell item carefully back in its place. "Everything is a competition with men, and if they aren't first, then they're last. Women are wired differently. At least, most women are."

"Which way are you wired?"

"Me?" Her brows collided above her nose. "I guess I'm more competitive than most. My research is cutting edge, and I definitely want to be the first in my field."

"And when you've done what you've set out to do?"

Her shoulders rose and fell. "I don't know. I suppose I'll find something else to focus on."

She went down on her knees again, this time attaching wires to the pads at his ankles. He clenched his hands into fists and focused on the flickering fluorescent light overhead. Looking at the top of her head brought to mind too many things *he'd* rather she focus on, and that road was filled with potholes deep enough to swallow his career.

Get your mind out of the gutter, man. He racked his brain for something to think about less likely to get him banned from the League. *What's the formula for earned run average? Number of earned runs divided by number of innings pitched then multiply by nine. So my ERA this year is…?* Not knowing his own stats was reason enough to bench his ass, if not trade him. No wonder he had been chosen as the guinea pig. "Fuck!"

Dr. Reed sprang to her feet, concern and contrition in every line of her face. "Did I pinch you?"

"No. Sorry. I'm fine, really. How much longer is this going to take?"

"One more wire then it will take a few minutes to connect to my computer, and we'll be good to go."

"Go where, exactly? No one's told me anything, except to show up here today. What do you hope to learn from all this?" He swept his hand through the air to indicate her handiwork.

She grabbed another wire from the pile on the desk and circled around behind him. He twisted to watch her lean over and clamp the wire onto a pad at the base of his spine. As she righted herself, her knuckles brushed over his left cheek. It was barely contact, but he felt it all the way up his spine to the tips of his ears. Ever on alert for opportunity, his cock twitched. The sizzle of electricity humming through his body had nothing to do with the wires attached to his body and everything to do with the woman wiring him up like a marionette.

He wanted her.

He hadn't wanted another woman since Hannah walked

out on him.

Jesus.

He was going to have to figure out another way of doing this without her touching him. Otherwise, he was going to carry out an experiment of his own. *How many times can I make her scream in an hour?*

"Mr. Walker didn't fill you in on the basis of my research?" She talked while she dug around in her bag again, coming out this time with something resembling the controller for the model railroad set he'd had when he was kid, only this one could run all the trains going out of Grand Central Terminal.

"No." Truth. Doyle seemed to be as in the dark as anyone. Why else would he have asked Royce to spy on her research? He eyed the sinister looking box while she collected the ends of his wires and popped them into the color-coded receptacles. "What's the Frankenstein box for?"

"Oh. I'm sorry. I should explain." She waved him closer. "This is a transformer, of sorts."

"Oh, hell, no!" He grabbed at the wires, succeeding in pulling a couple free before her laughter stopped him. His loyalty to the sport only went so far. "What?"

Damn. Her face lit up like Reunion Tower when she smiled. He couldn't help it, he smiled back. "What?" he repeated, laughing at himself now, too. "You're laughing at me?"

"What did you think I was going to do to you? Shock you?"

He gestured toward the box with the wires dangling from his fist. "That's what it looks like. You gonna tell me it's not what it looks like?"

"I promise you, it's not what it looks like." She pried his fist open then punched the ends back into the box before reaching behind it. Seeing the USB connection on the end eased his anxiety somewhat.

"I'm still not convinced you aren't going to electrocute me."

"Royce." His name rolled off her lips again, and he had a

ridiculous urge to hear her say it when he was buried deep inside her. "This plugs into my computer. The box gathers data from the electrodes attached to your body, translates the information into graphs and other data sets, then sends it all to my computer for further analysis."

"So, what are you expecting to learn from all of this?"

"My goal is to map your body at rest, and in routine motion, walking, sitting, stretching. Things you usually do. I'll gather data while you work, too, which in your case is playing baseball. By comparing the various sets of data, I hope to identify ways to maximize your potential on the field by determining which muscles or muscle groups are either under too much stress or underachieving. If my theories hold true, I might be able to help you overcome whatever physical factors are affecting your on-field performance."

He was speechless, which apparently, Dr. Reed took for interest in her project as she continued to talk. He picked up a few words. Theorem. Prototype. Groundbreaking. There were a host of others that sailed over his head like a homerun ball, high, fast, and impossible to catch.

Head spinning from information overload, he cut her off in mid-sentence. "Whoa! I don't give a rat's ass about any of those things. What I want to know is, what does it have to do with me?"

"I told you. You can't fix something you can't see. I understand you aren't playing up to your potential. I believe the data I collect will show me where you are failing, and from there, we can work to improve your performance."

"Sounds like a lot of bullshit to me."

"I've spent four years of my life developing the hardware and software for this prototype. If the trials produce the results I expect, then I plan to market the system to sports teams worldwide. The money made off those sales will be used to provide free units to hospitals and military rehab centers. So you see, Mr. Stryker, it's not bullshit to me."

God, she was sexy when she was riled up! The civilized part of him hated that he'd pushed her buttons, but a more primal part was damn glad he did. He'd been too tuned-in to the passion in her voice to pay attention to what she said, but he got the gist of it. She was out to change the world, and he was her next step toward her goal. He could live with being a research subject, as long as there was no more bloodletting and electric shocks involved.

"Okay, okay. Simmer down." It would be a shame if she did. He liked watching her breasts rise and fall with her rapid breaths. Hell, he hadn't seen anything as entertaining in…forever, it seemed. But Miss Prissy Scientist was off limits. "Let's just get this over with. What do you need me to do?"

"Nothing. Just stand there, for now." She resumed hooking him up, jamming the business end of the wires into her machine like she was shoving needles into a voodoo doll. He would have laughed, but he still wasn't sure she couldn't flip a switch and turn him into a roman candle. Instead, he indulged in a bit of fantasy, allowing his brain to take him places he physically couldn't go. She'd convinced him of her identity, but just because she was who she said she was didn't mean she wasn't connected to someone on the team.

"Why baseball?"

"It's a non-contact sport, most of the time. The tech who designed the wireless electrodes for me insisted they weren't ready for the kind of abuse they'd suffer in a full contact sport like football. He's working to fix the problem."

She inserted the last wire and turned to him. "All set. I'll connect to my computer then I'm going to ask you to go through some simple motions so I can see if all the electrodes are working properly."

He held his breath while she inserted the USB connection into a slot on her laptop. When no sparks flew, he blew the breath out.

After clicking away on the keyboard for a few minutes, she smiled up at him. "So far, so good. We'll start with your left arm. Raise it over your head slowly. Hold it there for the count of ten then lower it back to your side."

He hardly noticed the pad attached to his biceps, but the

one on his forearm was another story. As his muscles shifted, so did the skin covering them. For the first time since she suggested he take the time to shave, he wished he'd listened to her. The pad tugged uncomfortably on hair follicles, and he could only imagine how painful removing the pad would be. Refusing to let her see his discomfort, he concentrated on keeping his facial expressions neutral.

CHAPTER FOUR

He'd never again complain about a woman not waxing her lady parts. Shit, those pads had hurt coming off, just like Smarty Pants Scientist had said they would. He spread lotion on his now, smooth-as-a-baby's-butt skin, taking extra care with the patches where the hair had been ripped out by the roots. Shaving was the way to go, and though he'd been through a couple of razor blades getting rid of his body hair, he deemed the cost well worth it. Ripping those pads off had brought tears to his eyes. After removing the first two himself, he'd given up and had Dr. Reed yank the rest off, one after the other, as fast as she could. There had been no use prolonging the agony, he'd just wanted it over with.

To give her credit, she hadn't said, "I told you so." She'd even pretended not to see the tears he'd swiped away before they could spill down his cheeks.

Arriving at the stadium early, he grabbed his practice uniform from his locker and headed to her office. He'd change clothes in the trainer's restroom to avoid the razzing awaiting him when his teammates noticed his extreme manscaping.

Being a lab rat was bad enough without being the brunt of a million jokes. He couldn't hide it from them for long, but he'd take whatever reprieve he could get.

At the sound of the door opening, Tricia glanced up from the printout of yesterday's data she was studying. Royce Stryker stood there dressed in a Royal blue Mustangs T-shirt and loose fitting shorts hanging almost to his knees. Below the hem of his shorts, his legs were hairless. She tried not to smile, but failed. He'd come back! And, he'd taken her advice and shaved. She'd felt sorry for him yesterday, even if his discomfort had been because of his stubbornness.

"Hi."

"Hi, yourself," she said. Arranging her reports into a neat stack, she slipped them into the folder that would be their home until she got around to putting them into a binder. "Ready for a test run of the wireless system?"

"I suppose so." He crossed the room and set his duffle bag on a chair. He turned to face her, arms stretched out to his sides. "My body is yours."

Even though she knew his words weren't meant in a sexual way, they still caused every nerve ending in her body to tingle. She'd lain awake the previous night, imagining what it would be like to touch Royce in very non-clinical ways. When she'd finally closed her eyes and slept, she'd dreamt of him. Or rather, she'd dreamt of the two of them, doing things. Call her perverse, but ever since he'd threatened to spank her yesterday, before he knew who she was, she hadn't been able to get the thought out of her mind.

She wasn't a virgin, but she wouldn't call herself well tutored in sexual matters either. She knew just enough to understand some women liked to be spanked, that it was an aphrodisiac for them. Apparently, she was one of them.

This morning, she'd woken, aroused and wiggling her ass

in the air—something she'd been doing moments before in her dream while her imaginary lover brought his hand down on her bottom, over and over again. She'd been so damn horny, she'd reached for the vibrator in her nightstand to finish what her dream lover had started.

"Give me a sec." Thankful she'd left her bag on the floor beside the desk, Tricia bent to retrieve it, taking her time before lifting it to the desk. All she needed was a few seconds for her face to return to normal. She had no idea how to explain the color heating her cheeks to Royce. *Oh? You noticed the blush? It's nothing. I was just wishing you would spank me.*

Yeah, that would be professional. He'd report her to the Mustangs' management, and she'd be gone in a heartbeat. There wouldn't be another professional sports team who would touch her with a ten-foot cattle prod afterward.

Imagining the career-ending scenario turned her blood to ice, effectively putting a quick end to her erotic thoughts.

She dropped the bag on the desk then stood in order to get a better look at the contents. It didn't take long to find the small box of adhesive pads and the plastic container filled with what she would forever think of as electronic sperm.

"Take your shirt off, please." While he undressed, she found the page in her notebook where she had assigned numbers to each electrode frequency. Earlier, she'd used a marker to label the pad with corresponding numbers, all so she could keep track of what body part the data stream was coming from and match it against the baseline data. It wouldn't do to get her wires crossed, so to speak.

When she turned around. The sight of his bare chest stole the breath from her lungs. "Wow." She couldn't take her eyes off the wide expanse of light-gold skin. The absence of hair didn't make him look any less masculine, if anything, it made his shoulders appear wider and brought the definition in his abs front and center. She licked her lips, wanting to run her tongue along the deep valleys to scoop up the deliciousness of Royce Stryker.

"Like it?" He ran his hands over his hairless torso. "I

haven't been this smooth since I hit puberty. It feels good."

His voice jolted her back to reality, and she realized she'd been staring openmouthed at him like an awestruck teenager.

"I don't know how much trouble it's going to be to keep it this way, but we'll see. If I don't like it after a month, I'll just let it grow back. I tell you, I have a new appreciation for what women go through. I almost killed myself in the shower trying to shave my legs."

An image of Royce, naked with soapy water following the contours of his body, formed in her mind and wouldn't go away. Lord, what a sight that would be. "I hope you didn't cut yourself. What with your aversion to blood…."

A shudder racked his body. "I cut myself a couple of times." He raised his left leg, so he could point out a thin red line below his knee. "This one's going to leave a scar, I think."

She laughed at his theatrics. "If every little cut left a scar, there wouldn't be an unblemished woman on the planet."

"I might need stitches," he said, in all seriousness. Another shudder rippled over his magnificent pectorals.

Before he could become any more melodramatic, Tricia peeled the backing off the first pad, adhering it just above his left nipple with a smack. "I don't have a medical degree, but I predict you'll live. Would you like me to have the team doctor take a look, just to make sure?"

"No." He rubbed his chest where she'd all but slapped him. "What did you do that for?"

Four distinctive red marks indicated where her fingers had touched his skin. Once again, her mind shifted to her erotic dream the previous night. The marks on his chest were fading rapidly, but she didn't think his handprints on her ass would disappear as quickly. No, she was certain, even after they eventually did fade into oblivion, they would remain in her memory for the rest of her life.

"Let's focus on getting you ready to play today, okay?" She slapped another pad on his right pectoral with less enthusiasm than before. Nevertheless, she didn't let her fingertips linger. Even through brief contact, his newly-revealed skin was smooth and incredibly warm to the touch. And tempting. "I don't want team management complaining about you being late."

The woman had no appreciation for what he'd been through. Hell, he could have died in the shower last night. The sight of blood streaming down his leg after he'd sliced himself had almost done him in. If he hadn't grabbed hold of the handle on the back of the glass door and used it to steady himself while he collapsed against the wall, he might have broken his neck. Or bled to death. Luckily, clamping a washcloth over the wound had stopped the bleeding, or he would have been in big trouble.

But, he'd survived, and been more careful shaving his chest and arms over the sink. He'd rather clean up a mess than die in the shower.

Dr. Reed knelt at his feet in order to adhere pads to his legs. He glanced down, intrigued by the swell of her breasts visible down the front of her V-necked Mustangs shirt. Beneath the thin cotton, she wore a plain looking bra that lifted her assets up high, giving her cleavage he didn't remember seeing the day before. He would have remembered. A guy didn't forget creamy swells like hers, especially when the woman wasn't deliberately doing anything to show them off. If she'd been blatant about it, he wouldn't have given them a second look, but because she obviously didn't know how tantalizing they looked from his angle, he couldn't take his eyes off them. He flexed his hands, imagining how the feminine globes would feel.

Soft fingers slid beneath the hem of his shorts, lifting the fabric to expose his thigh. Already on the flight deck, his libido shot off the end of the runway into full-flight. Luckily, the woman causing all the commotion in his shorts was busy searching one-handed through the box of adhesive pads on the floor beside her. Royce stepped back.

Toppling forward, Tricia screeched, recovering her balance a split second before she would have face-planted on the floor.

Shit. His erection withered instantly. "I'm sorry." He crouched to her level. "Are you okay?"

She sat back on her heels and glared at him. "I'm fine." One hand rested on her thigh while she used the other to brush a lock of hair out of her face that had escaped her low ponytail. "Why did you move?"

He didn't dare tell her the truth, but if they were going to do this every day for a month, hiding his natural reaction to her wasn't going to be possible. It wasn't like he could control *that* part of his body, not when she touched him like the way she was. Perhaps, if she had a clue…. "You…. I mean…your hand was…." He closed his eyes, searching for a way to tell her that didn't make him sound like a pervert. Coming up empty, he opened his eyes.

She was looking at him as if he'd lost his mind, and maybe he had. This whole thing was insane anyway, so why sugarcoat it. He took a deep breath then let the words fly. "When you touched me, I got an erection."

The stunned look on her face would have been comical if his job hadn't been on the line. If she reported him for sexual harassment, he wouldn't have to worry about getting his mojo back. Mustangs' management would kick his ass to the parking lot in a heartbeat.

"But, I touched you yesterday."

He could practically see the cogs turning inside her analytical brain as she worked out what he was saying. "Yesterday was different. Don't ask me how, 'cause I can't tell you. All I know is, when you slid your hand under my shorts…. It was a natural reaction."

"I see." She grabbed the two boxes on the floor containing her stuff and stood. "Well. I've got to put the electrodes on you."

Royce stood his ground while she stared at him with narrowed eyes. He held her gaze, refusing to let her see him sweat. Did she even know she held his fate in her hands?

"Take your shorts off."

"What?!" Of all the things he imagined her saying, take it off wasn't even on the list.

"It's the shorts. Putting my hand inside your clothing is too intimate, so the solution is to take them off."

"But…."

"You didn't have the same reaction yesterday, did you?"

"Um." He looked down at his feet.

"You did?" Her voice had raised a couple of octaves, enough to nearly pierce his eardrums.

He returned his gaze to hers. "It didn't last long." He'd had too much on his mind yesterday, what with the blood test and everything else she'd sprung on him. Sexual attraction had taken a backseat.

"I don't believe this." She fisted her hands on the curve of her hips. She looked furious and flummoxed, all at the same time, and damn if her reaction wasn't sexy.

His cock stirred again. This time, he refused to shield his reaction. It wasn't like she was the kid he'd first thought she was. She was a grown woman, a scientist no less. She knew the way of the world, and she had to know how men reacted to her. "What can I say? I'm a man, and you're an attractive female."

He thinks I'm attractive?

The thought warmed her from the inside out. She wrapped the feeling up with a mental ribbon to be examined later. She'd promised to have Royce ready in time for batting practice, and she wasn't going to fail on her first day. *Why can't he act like nothing was wrong?* Why did he have to bring his problem out into the open? As long as they both pretended not to notice then they wouldn't have to address the issue. But, nooooo. Mr. Too Sexy to Ignore had to go and blow the lid off the proverbial pot.

Now, his lack of control was out there, so to speak, and they'd have to deal with it before they could move on.

The college kids she'd worked with had all the decency to pretend nothing was going on when they reacted to her touch.

She'd expected reactions from the younger men, had braced herself to pretend she didn't notice, but she'd expected someone of Royce's age and experience to have better control over his desire. That he didn't, thrilled her. Not that she wanted him to know how he affected her. She needed his complete cooperation, and if he got a whiff of her attraction to him, she'd lose whatever respect she might have garnered thus far.

"Look. All I'm saying is, yesterday, you seemed to deal with me touching you just fine. Maybe if you weren't wearing so many clothes...."

One eyebrow rose on his handsome face. "That's your theory? I'm wearing shorts?"

"It's all I've got." She drummed her fingers on the desk. "If you aren't wearing clothes, I won't be sticking my hands inside them."

"Makes sense to me."

She tried not to look. She really did. But from the moment he hooked his thumbs into the elastic waistband and began to push his shorts down, she became incapable of not looking. The first inch revealed a line of demarcation clearer than the Mason-Dixon Line between the shaved and au natural portions of his body. The shortened arrow disappeared beneath the briefest pair of briefs she'd ever seen. He turned just a fraction, and her breath caught in her lungs.

Holy crap! His ass was bare! "That's a—"

"Jock strap," he supplied as if there wasn't anything but some elastic straps and a scrap of fabric between her and his genitals. She watched helplessly as he cupped his package, adjusting the mass to suit him.

His erection strained at the stretchy red fabric. As painful as she imagined his predicament to be, it couldn't compare with what was going on inside her. Her breasts were heavy with need, her nipples aching to escape the confines of her practical cotton bra. Every nerve ending between her navel and her knees felt like they'd been hooked up to an electrical current.

Intellectually, she understood her response was instinctive. Women were hardwired to respond to the virile, alpha male, and no one fit the bill better than the man standing before her. As much as mankind wanted to pretend they'd risen above their baser instincts, the two of them were proof that nothing had changed since the dawn of man.

Intellect didn't have a chance against primal instinct. She should write a paper on the subject, but doing so would set the women's movement back several centuries and kill her respectability in the scientific world, so she'd keep her observations to herself.

Royce straightened, wadded his shorts into a ball, and tossed them NBA-style toward his duffle bag. "Two points!"

His exclamation snapped her out of her lust-fueled haze. Damn the man for looking the way he did. How was she supposed to function with him short-circuiting her nervous system? But function, she would. She had to. There was simply too much on the line to contemplate failure.

"Bravo." She grabbed the last pad and peeled the backing away. "Think you can hold still while I finish up?" Not waiting for an answer, she slapped the final pad onto his left thigh. She was careful this time to make sure there was no skin to skin contact.

He jerked backwards, his hands coming around in a protective gesture. "Shit. You should warn a guy before you touch him there."

Tricia grabbed a couple of wireless electrodes. How the hell she planned to work the tiny electrodes into the slots without making physical contact was going to be another thing. Attaching the flimsy wires required a delicate touch. The prototypes were too expensive to take chances with.

"Your manhood is safe." As the lie tripped off her tongue, she gestured for him to come closer. Every minute they spent together, the safety of his manhood became more of an issue. "Come over here." She pointed to the floor right in front of her.

Dropping his hands to his sides, he resumed his position in front of her.

Royce held his arms out wide, his gaze sweeping their length then down his torso to his feet. "I look like a prickly pear cactus." Little wires stuck out of the pads attached to his body like cactus needles and looked just as dangerous. "How the hell am I supposed to wear my uniform, much less play baseball with all this crap on me?"

"The wires are flexible, but if you want, I can tape them down. Just the ends need to be exposed in order to transmit signals."

Taping them meant she'd have no choice but to touch him. As much as he liked the idea, he didn't know if he could take much more skin-to-skin contact. She was driving him out of his mind. Slowly. One touch at a time.

He never would have agreed to participate in this experiment if he'd known the process involved getting naked and standing still while the hottest scientist in the universe put her hands all over him.

Any other time, having her touch him wouldn't be a problem. Hell, he'd give her directions a blind person could follow. But this? This was torture. Pure and simple. Royce fisted his hands in his hair and, with teeth clenched tight, he tugged hard on his scalp. The pain didn't solve anything, but it did help him focus on something other than his dick. The wayward appendage had found a target and wasn't going to give up on it easily. Still, time was running out. He needed to get his uniform on and get the hell out on the field before someone came searching for him. One last look confirmed his decision. "Tape them down. I can't go out there looking like I had a run-in with a porcupine."

"Okay. Hold out your hands, fingers spread." She tore off strips of athletic tape, sticking them to the ends of his fingers. One by one, she peeled off a piece and used it to secure a wire. When she'd used all ten, she repeated the process. Hair or no hair, playing with crap stuck to his body wasn't going to be fun. And taking it off at the end of the day was going to be hell.

Five minutes later, she stood back, hands on her hips, to admire her work. "All done. You can get dressed now."

It was easier said than done, but Royce managed to get his uniform on over the experimental equipment. He was ready to head out the door when she stopped him.

"Wait. Let me see if I'm getting a signal from all the receptors."

He glanced at the clock mounted on the wall. "No time. You'll have to do it while I stretch and take batting practice." He was out the door before she opened her laptop. There was only so much a man could stand, and he'd reached his limit for the day. Hell, for the century.

"And I only have to do it twenty-nine more times," he mumbled as he pushed through the locker room door and came face-to-face with the team captain, Jason Holder.

"Hey, man. Where ya been?"

If management hadn't told the captain what was up, Royce damn sure wasn't going to mention it. He let the lie roll off his tongue without thinking twice. "Training room. Coach thought it might help to get in some extra stretches before the game."

Jason clapped him on the back. "Whatever works for you. If you've been stretching, then you're probably ahead of the rest of us." He pulled the door open. "Take your time."

Royce sat down on the chair in front of his locker. Taped skin protested every move he made, but he managed to get his cleats on and grab his glove. Maybe once he got out on the field, had something else to occupy his mind, he'd forget about how uncomfortable he was. Like having a blister on your heel. It's annoying and painful, but you have to walk, so you learn to live with it. Pleased with his reasoning, he slipped his hat on and went out to take some warm-up throws.

CHAPTER FIVE

As soon as the door closed behind Royce's magnificent ass, Tricia sank into the desk chair. Her elbows came down on the desktop, her palms perfect supports for her head which seemed to weigh ten tons all of a sudden.

Royce Stryker was going to be the death of her. No doubt about it.

"This is only the second day," she muttered. "I'll never survive a month without losing my mind." She squeezed her eyes shut at the same time she clenched her thighs together, seeking relief from the insistent throbbing in both places. *Headache brought on by sexual frustration.* That was one for the record books. Had any clinical studies been done on the subject? If not, she could start one. She already had a test subject—her.

Day one. Subject exhibits signs of sexual attraction. Wet palms, dry mouth alternating with periods of drooling, slight tremors along extremities, shortness of breath. Typical signs of arousal noted—pebbled nipples, swollen genitalia, and excessive fluid secretion. Aching.

Day two. Subject can't keep her eyes off male subject's cock. Tremors are more pronounced, possibly interfering with subject's ability to do her job. Irrational daydreaming bordering on delusional fantasies. All other symptoms noted previously remain constant, if not elevated. Subject reports throbbing sensation behind her eyes that seems to be linked to a matching, though no less painful feeling in her genitals. Symptoms abate somewhat when male subject is removed from the room, but do not altogether disappear.

Day three. Subject died of mortification and/or sexual frustration.

Tricia groaned. She let her forehead drop to the desk, giving in to the weight of self-pity dragging her down. Royce's physical response was nothing more than primal instinct. She understood the reaction on a professional level, but on a personal level she wanted to believe the man was as affected by her as she was by him. It was nothing but pure feminine vanity on her part, but there it was. Proof that deep down inside she was just like every other woman on the planet. She wanted a man to see her for who she was, not just a convenient receptacle to appease his sexual needs.

If she gave Royce any indication she was attracted, she felt certain the man would scratch her itch. She wasn't exactly a troll, and he did react to her touch.

As quickly as the thought entered her head, she pushed it right back out. Sanity returned in direct proportion to her ebbing arousal.

I've got a job to do. Just do it, and get the hell out of here. Royce was only the first of dozens of sexy athletes she'd have to touch before she collected enough data to make her research viable. No doubt, he wasn't the last who would have a physical reaction to her touch, or the last she would find sexually attractive.

I can't sleep with all of them.

Strike that. I can't sleep with any *of them.*

End of story.

If word got out she was sleeping with the players she was supposed to be using as human guinea pigs, she'd be shut down faster than she could say, "You're out!" She couldn't let that happen. She'd worked too hard, and sunk everything she had into the project, to blow it now.

She'd just have to put on her clinical blinders and get the job done.

Having talked herself back to sanity, Tricia lifted her head. She was supposed to be out there now, monitoring the data stream instead of sitting here having a single woman with a demanding career pity party. Inhaling deeply, she held the breath for the count of three then let it out in a whoosh. "Time to go."

"Fuck." Royce cursed under his breath. He rolled his shoulders then stepped back into the batter's box and tried to concentrate on the easy practice pitches coming his way. This was when he should be focusing on the mechanics of his swing. No one expected a pitcher to actually hit the ball, but he didn't want to look like a complete idiot when it was his turn. And heck, if he could help the team on offense, he was all for it. The zillion adhesive patches stuck to his body were constant reminders of his less-than-human status. He'd been relegated to the level of a lab rat, his every movement recorded and analyzed. Hell, he couldn't even take a piss without a certain gorgeous researcher knowing about it.

Even knowing the next pitch would be right over the plate, he still swung and missed.

"You got somewhere else to be, Strikeout?"

Royce glared at the rookie first baseman. "That's Mr. Stryker to you, lefty." The last thing he needed was shit from a kid who still needed help wiping his ass.

"One more, Royce." This from Jake Tulleson, the Mustangs' batting coach, who stood behind the portable backstop. "We've got a lot of guys waiting."

Translation, get the hell out of the way so the guys who actually score runs can get some practice. He could take a hint. His time was better served getting to know the batters he would face than trying to perfect his swing.

He managed to put some lumber on the next throw, sending the ball in a lazy arch any idiot could see would be an instant out during the game. *Oh well.*

"Hey, man." Jason Holder stopped him on the way to the dugout.

"Hey." Royce studied his foot as if digging holes in the crushed granite track was the most fascinating thing in the world. It sure beat the hell out of meeting the team captain's gaze. Jason had led the League in batting for the last several years, and judging by the group at the railings trying to get his attention, he was a crowd favorite.

Jason waved to his adoring fans. "Give me a minute," he called out, and the group went silent.

"Don't keep 'em waiting on my account."

"They'll keep." Jason put a hand on Royce's back, turning them both so the fans couldn't see their faces. "I don't have a clue what's going on with you, man, but whatever it is, it'll pass. They don't call you Strikeout for nothing."

"You and I both know I couldn't strikeout Helen Keller right now. No sense trying to make this something it isn't."

"It's a slump, Strike. Everybody has 'em. Trust me, I know. Been there, done that. It was all in my head, as it turns out."

He vaguely remembered a few seasons back when Jason couldn't have hit a soccer ball if it had been pitched to him. "What did you do? I mean, how did you fix it?"

His teammate shrugged. "I got my head screwed on straight, if you get my meaning?"

"You got laid?" It couldn't be that simple, and the idea of Jason Holder being sexually inactive was ludicrous. Before they'd gotten married, he and his twin brother, Jeff, had been two of the most eligible bachelors in the state of Texas.

"Shh!" He glanced around to make sure no one had heard Royce's question. Assured they were out of hearing range, he continued. "In a manner of speaking, yes. Look, you haven't been on your game since your divorce. This is all conjecture on my part, and I realize your personal life is none of my business.

The team needs you to be at your best, Strike." He clapped Royce on the shoulder. "We've got your back, man, but whatever is going on, you've got to figure out how to fix it." Jason steered him toward the waiting fans. "Come on. Put a smile on your face and let's sign some stuff for the kids."

Most of the fans hanging on the rail were there to see Jason, but there were a few who would be happy with an autograph from anyone, even him. Royce followed the Mustangs' catcher, even allowed him to pass a few things on for him to sign, too. The fans he made eye contact with seemed pleased to have met him which went a long way toward lifting his spirits. But deep inside, he felt as if a chunk of him was missing.

He'd lost his ability to play the game he loved. Would possibly lose his job if he didn't get his shit together soon. As if those two things weren't enough, he had the hots for someone he absolutely could not touch.

Dr. Tricia Reed was off limits. Career suicide.

The crowd thinned. Royce signed a pink baseball cap for a little girl with twinkling blue eyes, blonde pigtails, and missing front teeth. A boy, perhaps ten years old, put his arm around her. "Come on, sis. Dad's waiting."

The girl took three steps before turning back to wave good-bye. As he returned her wave, he felt as if a giant hole had opened up beneath his feet. Scanning the seats farther up, he found what he was looking for. A guy dressed in cargo-style shorts, a Mustangs' T-shirt and cap, smiled down at the kids. Pride and love etched the man's face. Ever since his wife had left him, Royce had been thinking the only thing he'd lost had been a spouse, but suddenly, everything became crystal clear.

The man in the stands had what Royce wanted for himself. A family. He wanted kids—a boy he could teach to play baseball—hell, a girl he could teach to play baseball. Girls could play, too. He wanted to buy pink baseball caps and toy trucks and bicycles.

Back when they were young, he and Hannah talked about having kids, but after his career took off, the time had never seemed right. The conversation had died right along with the marriage.

"Take some time before the game to relax. Leave your personal problems in the locker room." Jason's voice snapped Royce back to the present.

He turned away from the stands, letting his gaze sweep over the field. He wasn't ready to leave baseball any more than he'd been ready to dissolve his marriage. But one thing was for certain, he was damn sure going to put up more of a fight before he gave up his career.

Keeping his head down, he ducked into the dugout and headed straight for the tunnel connecting to the clubhouse.

Everyone else was out on the field or working with the trainers, so he had the place to himself. He left his cleats in his locker, grabbed a water bottle from the cooler, and flopped down in one of the comfortable chairs in the players' lounge. He needed a few minutes to himself, a few quiet minutes to get his head on straight before the game.

His agent had suggested he try some meditation techniques, had even sent over some videos Royce had thrown in the trash without ever watching them. But with a picture of the family he would never have running through his mind, complete with Jason's voice telling him he needed to get laid, Royce was in desperate need of something to help him focus on the game.

After taking a long drink from his water bottle, he capped it then trapped it between the back of the chair and his neck, the muscles tightening against the cold before he willed them to relax. He closed his eyes and did his best to recall line-for-line the scouting report he'd read earlier on the team that he would face in a couple of hours. It wasn't long before the information faded, and something—rather—someone took its place.

Eyes as green as the outfield and golden hair that reminded him of the sun setting over the bleachers in right-center field. Breasts like twin pitching mounds, front and center, not intrusive, but big enough to make the landscape interesting. He had bats longer than her legs, but not near as shapely. And her ass—he could see her draped over the dugout fence, her sweet backside naked and begging for him to slap it with his glove a few times until it turned Mustangs red.

"Wake up, Strike. There's some woman in the hall says she needs to see you."

Royce woke with a start. He rubbed the heels of his hands into his eye sockets in an effort to scrub the last image away.

"You okay?" Jeff Holder, the Mustangs' ace closer stood over him.

Royce reached for his cap, relief flooding him when he realized it was still in his lap. The last thing he needed was for a teammate to see him sporting a boner before a start. "I'm fine. Just visualizing the game."

Jeff nodded as if what Royce had said sounded perfectly logical. "Can't hurt, I guess. Whatever it takes to get the job done."

The veteran player headed toward the cooler stocked with water bottles. Tossing his half-empty water bottle into the trash, Royce briefly considered grabbing another one. Nothing short of an ice pack in his pants was going to make the reminder of his fantasy go away. Not with the subject of the dream waiting for him in the hall.

"Hey!"

He paused with his hand on the door handle and looked over his shoulder at the only other occupant of the room. Jeff stood with one hand on his hip, the other holding a water bottle poised halfway to his smiling lips. The future Hall of Famer could be a poster boy for Major League Baseball.

"Have fun out there, today."

Fun. Yeah, right. It was damn hard to have fun when your opponents were hitting the cover off every pitch you threw. Jeff understood. To take the man's comment as anything other than encouragement would be wrong. Like his twin brother, Jason, Jeff wasn't the kind of guy to throw sand in your face when you were down.

Royce forced a smile to his face and nodded. "I'll do my

best."

"That's all we ask."

I know. I just wish to hell my best wasn't shit. With that thought swirling around in his head, he jerked the door open.

Tricia leaned against the opposite wall, her laptop held in both hands so it covered her shorts. Her facial expression changed from boredom to something resembling interest when she recognized him, to annoyance faster than a summer squall crossing the plains.

"Lookin' for me?"

"There's a problem with one of the sensors."

"Which one?"

Her gaze dropped to his groin then jerked back up to his face. His conversation with Jeff had helped calm his libido, but seeing her eyes drift down his anatomy had him harder than cured maple again. "Left thigh."

He wasn't going to let her off so easy. He rubbed his leg while wishing he, or she, was rubbing something else. "Want me to drop my pants?"

Up. Down. Up. Down. Her gaze followed his hand as if he were hypnotizing her. He'd never tried mesmerizing a woman into bed with him. *You are growing sleepy. No, make that, you are growing horny. Spread your legs, let me taste you.*

That line of thought didn't help anything. His hand stalled, and she looked into his eyes.

"Well…maybe. I don't know. I need to see what's up…. I mean, I need to see why it isn't working."

Damn, she was cute when she was flustered. His fingers itched to feel the heat coloring her cheeks, to trail down her body to test the temperature of the rest of her. If he peeled her T-shirt off, would he find more rosy skin?

"Come on." He considered holding out his hand to her, but just waved her along as he turned and headed down the hallway. There was no time to seduce her. He had to get out to the bullpen to warm up.

She followed him to a small room stacked floor-to-ceiling with cases of water bottles and cardboard boxes containing

God only knew what. Stuff they used in the clubhouse, he assumed.

As the door swooshed closed behind her, her eyes went wide. "A supply closet?"

"Hey, it's private." He worked his belt loose followed by the waistband button then the zipper. "You didn't think I was going to let you grope me in the hallway, did you?"

"No." Her gaze was locked on the triangle made by his open britches. "I...."

He leaned back against a stack of boxes and spread his legs. "Do what you need to do. I've got to go to work."

She placed her laptop on a case of sports drinks then stepped forward. She moved as if she had pine tar stuck to the bottom of her shoes, all the while looking at his groin. His dick swelled until he was sure if she didn't get a move on, he would explode right there.

"I haven't got all day," he reminded her.

He should have made it easy on her. He should have pushed his pants to his knees, but he hadn't. She came closer. So close he could smell the floral scent on her hair. Below was an earthy scent that was all woman.

He was hard. Everywhere. He felt as if he'd turned to stone—living, breathing stone. While his body was frozen in limbo, his senses were painfully alive. The toe of her sneaker squeaked on the polished concrete floor. If he hadn't already been blind with lust, her halo of spun gold hair would have done the job.

Toe-to-toe with him, she pressed the tips of her fingers to his stomach. He sucked in a breath and held it as her tiny hand slid inside his uniform. She skimmed the elastic band of his jock strap then moved down past the crease where his hip and thigh joined. Everywhere she touched him, his flesh burned.

As her hand explored farther south, her body pressed closer to his until her breasts flattened against his ribcage. She turned her head so her cheek met his sternum, her cute little nose so close to his left nipple her breath made the tiny nub pucker and bead.

Royce ground his teeth until the pain in his jaw forced him to speak. "Stop!"

With one hand on the box behind Royce and the other not more than an inch from finding the malfunctioning electrode, Tricia froze. If anyone were to see them like this, both their careers would be over. Well, maybe not his, but hers would be. It was her hand down his open pants. Her cheek pressed to his heaving chest, her forearm planking next to his raging hard-on.

His hands were flattened against the box in a sort of reverse Spider Man death grip. He wasn't even touching her.

Embarrassment and shame washed over her followed by anger—at him for practically daring her to take his challenge, and at herself for doing so.

"I'm sorry." She peeled her face from his incredibly warm chest even as she began to extract her hand. Fingers like steel bands clamped around her forearm, stilling her movement.

"Don't. Move."

Once again, she froze. His labored breaths stirred the hair on the top of her head. She didn't dare look up at his face. Instead, she focused on his hand wrapped around her arm. She was fragile porcelain to his sturdy ironstone. As unbreakable as his grip was, it was gentle, too.

"I need a minute."

Along the length of her forearm, his penis had escaped the bounds of his jock strap. A trickle of scalding liquid trailed down her skin. She licked her lips, wanting suddenly to taste that drop of pre-cum, to taste all of him.

She tugged on her arm, and he let her go. All the reasons she should not do what she was about to do ricocheted around inside her skull. Before one of the tiny bullets of sanity lodged in her brain, she grasped the waistband of his uniform in both hands, and sinking to the floor, she took his pants down with her.

He reacted fast, but perhaps having so much blood pooled in his groin was a detriment to his athleticism because his hands were too late. By the time he grasped her head between his palms to stop her, she'd freed his cock and swallowed as much of it as she could.

"Christ Almighty!" he hissed, digging his fingers into her scalp.

Tricia hummed her agreement, earning another growled oath from his lips. She used her tongue to taste him, sweeping along his length then swirling around the bulbous head until he rewarded her with another drop of pre-cum. He smelled like he tasted, salty and pure male.

Addicting. For a second she gave in to the sheer panic of thinking she could not live without tasting this man again. Then one of those missiles of sanity lodged in her brain.

What am I doing?! She tried to pull away, but his big hands held her steady.

"Fuck, no. Finish it, Tricia. Fucking finish it."

Her heartbeat was bruising her ribs, pounding with enough force she thought the protective bones might crack.

Just this once. Never again. One time. For him. For me.

She wrapped the fingers of one hand around the base of his cock and braced her other against his hip. She'd only done this once before—in a car with a gearshift knob grinding into her tit and a steering wheel thumping against her skull. She'd been underage and stupid enough to believe the college senior when he'd said he cared about her. When she let his cum jettison onto his dress shirt, he'd called her a bitch and took her home.

This was different. She wanted to take Royce into her mouth. His desire was nothing more than a physical one, but it was one she returned wholeheartedly. She craved his scent, his taste, his strength. And when he took control, holding her head steady while he fucked her mouth, she submitted to him. He clearly knew what he was doing where she knew next to nothing.

He let go of her head with one hand long enough to force her fingers from his shaft, gently guiding them to his hip, silently encouraging her to hold on tight. She dug her nails into the rock-hard muscles as he drove his cock to the back of her throat.

Anatomy lessons were her friend. She remembered to breathe through her nose and relax the soft palette to lessen the gag reflex. He was big, but she was taking nearly all of him by the time he tensed and let go of her head, giving her the option to swallow his impending release or not.

There was no decision to make. She pulled his hips forward. The head of his cock hit the back of her throat. Royce's fingers bit into her scalp. Muffled curses exploded in the fetid air. Liquid heat bathed her tongue then slid down her esophagus. She worked the muscles in her throat, swallowing and draining him at the same time.

When his body relaxed a tiny fraction, telling her he was spent, she eased back on her heels. She couldn't bring herself to look at his face, but watched through her lashes as he righted his uniform, the wayward electrode still in need of repair.

She said nothing.

What could she say?

She'd literally blown her research project. On the second day.

"I've got to go. Do you want these back after the game?"

He meant the sperm-like electrodes. She shook her head, unable to explain that she had different ones to try out each day. She wouldn't be needing them now. He had every right to be angry. She'd used him. Not like he'd expected to be used, but in the most degrading manner and unprofessional way possible.

"I'll take them off myself, then. Meet me at the player gate after the game."

She remained on her knees long after he'd left, the door closing behind him with a decidedly final *kerthunk*.

CHAPTER SIX

He was so blind with rage he couldn't see where he was going.

He could still feel her lips on his dick, and damn, if he didn't want to feel her hot, wet heat again. He should have stopped her. It was all his fault. If he hadn't been an ass, had pulled his pants down and let her fix the damn electrode instead of making her sidle up close so she had to put her hand down his uniform.... But, Christ Almighty, he'd wanted to feel her hands on him, wanted to provoke her.

You did a damn fine job of it, asshole. If anyone had discovered them, the scandal would have ended both their careers.

After turning a corner that led to someplace in the bowels of the stadium, he sagged against the wall and sucked in a deep, cleansing breath. He had to get his shit together.

From where he was, he couldn't hear the crowds, but he could sense the energy building. In a few short minutes, he'd be expected to go out to the mound and pitch at least five innings. Six if he could manage. Seven if he got lucky.

He hadn't been lucky in months.

They called him Strikeout. Strike for short. But lately, the media had been more inclined to say Stryker had gone on strike. Like he'd deliberately quit striking batters out. He wished his problem was so simple. If it had been, he would just as deliberately begin striking them out again.

But it wasn't simple. It was complicated as hell. It seemed the harder he tried to throw strikes, the fewer he threw. Scratch that. He was throwing strikes alright. Right. Over. The. Plate. Down the middle. Right in the batter's wheelhouse.

Didn't matter who the batter was, or what kind of pitches they excelled at hitting. Everyone in the league had gotten a hit off him this season. Or so it seemed.

Royce wiped his brow with his sleeve. Sweat stung his eyes. He could thank the unseasonably hot temperatures for that, but the river running down his spine had nothing to do with the weather and everything to do with his state of mind. It was only the third inning, but he'd given up four runs and loaded the bases twice on a combination of walks and dinky hits. Some pitchers might blame the fielders for not making outs, but not him. Every one of the hits he'd given up had been legit. He had no one to blame but himself.

No way would Doyle bring in a new pitcher this early in the game, so Royce had no choice but to stick it out for as long as it took. Another two innings, maybe three before he could tuck his tail between his legs and skulk away.

He'd have plenty of time to think about escaping later. First, he had to get out of his current situation—hopefully, without giving up any more runs. Experience told him not to expect such a fortuitous outcome, so he shut off the voice of reason and tried to concentrate on the next pitch.

One pitch at a time. Nothing you can do about the runners standing on first and second so focus on getting this batter out.

Royce took a deep breath then let it out before wedging his right foot up against the pitching rubber and turning his head toward home plate. The ball felt natural as he held it lightly behind his back. He'd been here thousands of times in his career, he told himself. This was just one more day at the office.

Jason flashed a series of signs to indicate the pitch he expected Royce to throw.

Coming to a set, hands together in front, he visualized the pitch. His mind and body knew every minute detail—how to grip the ball, how hard to throw it, when to let it fly from his fingers. He saw the pitch in his mind's eye—saw it break before coming in over the outside corner of the plate for a strike. If he did everything just right, the ball would end up in Jason's mitt and not over the center-field wall.

If.

Over the last few months, *if* had become a very big word.

Royce willed the negative thoughts out of his brain. With runners on base, two outs, and two strikes on this batter, there was no room for anything but perfection.

Certain he had his head screwed on right, and everything from his brain to his toenails were in complete sync, he went into his wind-up. The ball flew from his fingertips only to soar back over his head like a guided missile a split-second later.

For every foot the ball traveled, his stomach sank a few inches. The Mustangs were behind seven runs, thanks to him, and there wasn't a damn thing he could do but stand there on the mound looking like a fool.

Tricia monitored the incoming data with little interest. Whatever had been wrong with the one errant transmitter had somehow fixed itself, though she had no clue how. Perhaps it had been nothing more than a bad connection and all the jostling of clothing when she gave Royce a blow job had done the trick.

She stifled a groan as the memory of what she'd done before the game flooded back in—for the zillionth time. No doubt, she'd managed to jiggle the tiny device back into working while she had her hands and mouth on a certain, not so tiny device.

And, she had the records to prove it.

Several minutes of the data stream told the story in clear, scientific detail. Elevated heart rate, tense muscles, skin temperature bordering on heat stroke. It was all there in graphs and numerical charts for the world to see.

If—no, make that, *when* Royce Stryker told the world what she'd done, there would be no way to deny it. She could delete those few minutes, but any good computer forensics person could drag it out from the bowels of hell in a matter of seconds. No point in even thinking about it. She'd meet Royce after the game, as decreed, and take her punishment like a woman.

In the meantime, she brought up the file she'd saved. What harm would it do to look at it now? The damage was long-since done and nothing would change it so she might as well enjoy the satisfaction of knowing she'd made his heart race and his blood pressure spike—among other things.

She closed her eyes, and the taste of him burst on her tongue all over again. As long as she lived, she'd never forget a single detail of that encounter. The way he'd tasted, his unique scent, the size of him stretching her lips, filling her, demanding she take all of him. She didn't really need the computer graphics to remind her, but she was damn sure going to print out a copy before Royce or the Mustangs or whoever made her destroy the information.

Without hesitation, she sent the documents to the remote printer she'd hooked up in her temporary office. She wouldn't have gone to the trouble of setting the device up if she'd known how temporary her situation would be.

In the top of the fifth inning, Doyle Walker, the Mustangs' manager, stalked out to the pitching mound. Royce was finished for the day, and none too soon, judging by the reaction of the fans. He'd managed to get through the fourth inning without giving up any more runs, but he walked the first two batters in the fifth, and that, apparently, had been enough.

Tricia let the data stream continue until Royce disappeared through the dugout to the clubhouse, then she shut the computer program down. His physical reaction to being removed from the game wouldn't be useful for her purposes. Neither was his reaction to getting a pre-game blowjob, which was why she decided to head back to her office and start packing her equipment.

He should have remained in the dugout with the rest of the team, but given his present mood, he didn't think anyone would call him out on it. Slumped in the chair in front of his locker, he tried to sort through the array of feelings swirling around inside him. Frustration rose to the top. He'd always prided himself on what he brought to the team, but he hadn't brought anything but crap in too long. At this rate, it was only a matter of time before they took him out of the rotation. A trade was out of the question. There wasn't a team in the League who would take him with his current stats. Which left the Minor League. If the Mustangs took him out of the rotation, they'd have to bring someone up from the Mavericks, their AAA farm team in Waco.

They'd make room on the forty-man roster by sending his ass down to God-only-knew where. He doubted the Mavericks would want him, so he'd probably end up riding the bench with some team down on the Mexican border until his contract expired.

Fuck. Getting his shit together had to be priority one.

So why was it the one thing he wanted most was to paddle Dr. Tricia Reed's ass?

She's a pain in my ass.

Since he was the only person in the locker room, he removed his shirt and undershirt and began ripping electrodes off his body. Even without hair, the process hurt like a son-of-a-gun. A month of this and he wouldn't have any skin left. All the more reason to end this project now. The sooner the woman was out of his sight, the sooner she would be out of his mind and he could go back to concentrating on saving his career.

Royce showered and dressed in record time. It was cowardly, but he wanted out of there before the game ended and the rest of the team came into the clubhouse. Unless a miracle occurred in the last half of the game, the Mustangs would lose, and the failure rested squarely on his shoulders. No one would dare say anything in the locker room, but for months, he'd heard the messages in his teammates' silence. If he listened closely, he could hear the minutes, hours, and days ticking away on his career.

A shadowed figure leaned against the concrete wall. *Royce.* Tricia's heart did a flip-flop before settling into a tap-dance-worthy rhythm she could only partially attribute to the man holding her career in his hands. The rest of her physical reaction to the Mustangs' pitcher was pure chemistry. Wrap testosterone up in a pretty package like Royce Stryker then dangle it in front of anything with an abundance of estrogen, and as they say, opposites attract.

The possibility of turning and going back to her office, locking the door, and staying there until the stadium emptied out crossed her mind. Reason screamed that taking the coward's route would only postpone the inevitable. At least if she met with him, perhaps she could convince him not to turn her in for sexual harassment. Maybe if she promised to keep her hands, and her mouth, to herself? Maybe if she apologized, explained to him how much her research meant to her, how much it could mean to people suffering from serious injury, not just athletes wanting to improve their game?

Squaring her shoulders, she approached the solitary man with caution. For all she knew, he would march her straight to the corporate offices and throw her into the pits of hell without so much as letting her utter a word in her defense.

You have no defense. What you did was offensive and aggressive, not to mention unprofessional. He has every right to demand to have you removed from the premises.

Wary of his stillness, she stopped a few feet away. Her footsteps had echoed in the barren hallway, so there was no possible way he didn't know she was there. Yet, he hadn't moved a muscle since she'd first spotted him. Her shaky resolve to take her punishment like a woman dissolved under an onslaught of reality.

Royce Stryker was a force to be reckoned with.

He wore a dark gray suit with a matching shirt that blended perfectly into the shadows. A tie, blue, perhaps, hung loose from beneath the starched collar he hadn't bothered to button. His hands bracketed his hips, the suit jacket hanging in the crook of his right arm. He seemed to be staring at a spot on the floor in front of him.

Uncertain what to do, Tricia waited. She'd thrown the first pitch in this battle. What became of it was up to him.

"We can't talk here."

Startled, Tricia barely heard his soft-spoken words.

She didn't think there was much to talk about. But if they were going to have it out, better to do it somewhere besides a stadium filled with forty thousand or so people. "No," she agreed.

"Is your car in the player's lot?"

"Yes."

He nodded then used his massive shoulders to push away from the wall. "We'll go to my place. It's private. You can follow me."

His place. Private. Where he could yell at her all he wanted and no one would hear. Then maybe, when he was through yelling, he'd let her plead her case. *Yeah, right.* "Okay."

His home was everything he said it was, though secluded

might have been a better description than private. The exclusive neighborhood screamed old money, where massive houses hid behind brick walls and electronic gates. Enormous trees that pre-dated the manmade structures shaded the streets and buckled with sidewalks only the hired help used. If you didn't have a car, you didn't belong was the unspoken statement.

After waving her through the gate that swung open at his approach, she watched in her rearview mirror as the wrought iron monstrosity closed behind her.

Trapped. In a cage of her own making. He led her around to the back of the three-story Grecian-style home where she parked beneath the limbs of an oak tree shading an enormous garage and bricked turnaround. If she hadn't known for a fact she was practically in the center of Dallas, she would have thought she'd been transported to a palatial estate in England or France.

As she stepped from her car, the peace and quiet of the area was both calming and disconcerting. It was as if the old-growth vegetation surrounding the estate swallowed up all the extraneous sound.

Someone touched her elbow, and she nearly jumped out of her skin. Even the moss-covered bricks acted as soundproofing. "I didn't hear you," she said, allowing him to lead her toward a glass-paned door on the back of the house.

"I bought this place because it's quiet."

Unnaturally so, she thought, but kept the observation to herself. Birds chirped in the trees, but even their songs seemed to be part and parcel to the stillness surrounding them. Truth be told, if she hadn't been apprehensive about what was to come, she would have loved the place. That a man like Royce Stryker lived here, surprised her. She'd taken him for a more modern type, had expected him to live in a McMansion in one of the up and coming suburbs. Instead, he lived smack-dab in the middle of *the* enclave of established Dallas society.

They entered through the kitchen—a warm and inviting room, despite its size. Tricia stopped, unable to credit the sheer magnificence. Her entire one-bedroom apartment would fit in this space alone.

"You live here by yourself?"

He tossed his keys into a pottery bowl sitting on a hand-painted console next to the door then reached for her purse. She let the strap slide off her shoulder, watched as he set her bag on the table, too. "Yep. I bought it after the divorce."

Some serious retail therapy. She kept the thought to herself. "I bet your wife would have loved it."

Ignoring her comment, Royce walked to a cabinet, and like magic, the façade swung open to reveal the practically barren interior of an industrial-size refrigerator. "I have beer and water."

She supposed the statement was an offer. "Water." She'd already proven she had no control when she was around this man. Alcohol could only make it worse.

He handed her a plastic bottle, grabbed one for himself then, without a word, headed toward another part of the house. Unscrewing the cap, Tricia tipped it to her lips. The cold liquid helped to ease the constant burn she felt inside when she was around Royce. As badly as she wanted to get back in her car and disappear for the next decade or so, she couldn't. He hadn't reported her—yet—which meant there still could be a chance to salvage her research, if not her career.

I'm sorry. I shouldn't have taken advantage of you. I promise I won't do it again. Please? Give me another chance?

She hadn't begged or pleaded since she was thirteen and got caught sneaking out of her room in the middle of the night in order to see a meteor shower. The words had fallen on deaf ears back then. She could only hope Royce Stryker was more forgiving.

If he said yes, she'd show him how to attach the electrodes himself so there wouldn't be any need for her to touch him— or even see him. It wasn't ideal. She'd lose something in the quality control, but at this stage of the game, she didn't see she had much choice. Beggars couldn't be choosers. With her new plan in mind, she felt better about the odds of convincing him to give her another chance. She twisted the cap back onto her water bottle and set out to find Royce.

CHAPTER SEVEN

Royce sat in his favorite chair, a big, overstuffed piece with a matching footstool he'd purchased especially for the den. He spent more time in this room than any other besides the bedroom, simply because the two rooms had furniture. One of these days, he'd get around to furnishing the rest of the rooms, but for now, he had everything a single man could need. He had a giant screen television, a satellite dish, some comfortable furniture to relax in, and he had a bed.

He didn't have a clue why he'd brought Dr. Reed to his house or what he was going to say to her now that she was here. She seemed wary of his intentions, but he hadn't imagined the light in her eyes when it came to his home. Her appreciation for his home went a long way to softening his anger toward her. He'd purchased the house, hoping it would bring Hannah back to him, but she'd taken one look and turned up her nose.

"It's old." Hannah wrinkled her nose in distaste.
It wasn't what she said, but how she'd said it, as if she couldn't

imagine why anyone would want an old house when they could have the new mini-mansion they'd purchased right after their move to Dallas. In his opinion, that structure lacked character, and no amount of age would give it any. For all its size and upgrades, it was still nothing more than an expensive tract home.

"I want more out of his living space," he told her. "I want hardwood floors, worn in the right places, and handcrafted woodwork. Not run-of-the-mill flooring and cheap pressed-wood moldings. I want quality that has already lasted a lifetime and will last for a few more."

She rolled her eyes at him and stormed off.

He'd thought Hannah was made of better stuff, but over time, her veneer had worn as thin as a hollow-core door. He couldn't blame her for everything that had gone wrong in their marriage. No, most of the blame rested on his shoulders. When they'd had no money to spend, Hannah had seemed content. She'd clipped coupons, bought off the sale rack, and furnished their cheap apartments with thrift store finds and build-it-yourself furniture.

Things had gone downhill when the money started pouring in and the demands of his career took more of his time. Suddenly, Hannah wanted to throw out everything old and replace it with new. He hadn't argued. Most of what they had was crap—but lovingly sought out and restored crap. When she'd pronounced the new house "finished", he realized he missed the personal touches of their previous home.

That's why he planned on spending the off season looking for the perfect furnishings for the rest of the rooms in his home. He already had a list of trade-day events, auctions, and antique stores he intended to visit. He wasn't a decorator, but he knew what he liked, and the hell with anyone who didn't approve. For once, he owned his own home, and when he was through with it, everything in it would be just the way he wanted it.

He'd almost forgotten about the woman he'd brought home until she appeared in the doorway looking as if she'd just fallen down the rabbit hole.

"There you are."

"I figured you would find me, eventually."

"You know, none of your rooms are furnished?" She sounded almost amused, definitely perplexed.

"I noticed."

"That one"—she pointed down the hall—"the dining room? It has the most amazing woodwork. Is it hand-carved walnut?"

She was his Kryptonite. He wanted to be mad at her. He *needed* to be mad at her, but knowing she valued the same things he did tempered his anger. He felt the stirrings of something very different—something he'd been fighting since he first laid eyes on her. But, she'd done something to jeopardize both their careers, and he couldn't continue to let that kind of behavior continue.

"It is."

The short answer seemed to take the wind out of her sails. He could almost see the instant she remembered what she'd done. Her shoulders slumped, and the light went out of her eyes. All her enthusiasm over vintage woodwork evaporated in an instant.

"Mr. Stryker—"

"Don't!" His barked command startled her, and she seemed to take a step back without actually moving. Damn. It was all he could do to remain seated when he really wanted to wrap her up in his arms and tell her everything would be all right. But, everything would not be fine. Not the way they were going. He lowered his voice. "Don't apologize for what you did."

"But…it was wrong." She couldn't have wrung another syllable out of the last word if she'd run it through a wringer washing machine. She sounded as young as she looked.

"Tell me again how old you are."

The change of subject caught her off guard, but only for a moment. "I'm twenty-five. Old enough to know better than to attack a man, especially in his place of employment. I promise—"

"Don't make promises you can't keep." The startled expression on her face confirmed what he already knew. The chemistry between them was too hot to ignore. She *would* have his dick in her mouth again. And he *would* fuck her every way he could think of. However, they weren't going to do it at the stadium.

Suddenly, he understood why he'd brought her to his home. He crooked his index finger at her. "Come here."

She took a few tentative steps forward then stopped.

"Closer," he urged until she stood perpendicular to his knees. He reached for her hand and she let him hold her fingers. "You behaved very badly today. If we'd been caught, we could have both lost our jobs."

She opened her mouth to say something, but a shake of his head and she pressed her lips into a tight line. He stroked his thumb over her knuckles. She was like a trapped animal, all wide-eyed and trembling. He knew the feeling. There was a lot at stake here. Not just their jobs, but so much more.

"I'm going to punish you for what you did then we won't speak of it again. Is my meaning clear?" For once, he'd stunned her speechless. "It's a simple question. Do you understand that I am going to punish you? Yes or no?"

"Yes. But—"

"You want to know how I'm going to punish you."

She nodded. She wasn't very articulate at the moment, but he would take his time. No one would disturb them tonight.

"I'm going to spank you, Tricia."

Her eyes widened, and she visibly shrank back from him.

He tightened his hold on her fingers—his only point of contact. If she wanted to run, she easily could. "You were a very bad girl, and you must be punished for your actions—by me or by someone else."

Royce waited for her to absorb the implications of his statement. If he told the team management what she'd done, she would be gone in the blink of an eye. Of course, he'd be gone, too, but she didn't have to know the Mustangs would assign more blame to him than to her.

"You aren't going to report me?" She couldn't have sounded more surprised if he'd told her he was going to strap a rocket to her back side and launch her to the moon.

"No. I intend to spank you until you can't sit down, then we'll forget today ever happened." At least the first part was true. The second half of his statement, not so much. He'd never had any kind of sex in a baseball stadium, unless he counted the time in high school when he'd coaxed the head cheerleader to the baseball field one night during a dance on campus. He'd copped a feel before she slapped him and left him standing in the visitor's dugout with a hard-on in his pants and the imprint of her fingers on his cheek. He hadn't forgotten, and he damn sure wasn't going to forget getting a blowjob in a supply closet minutes before he had to take the mound.

"I'm not a child." She'd regained some of her natural spunk. Good. But it wouldn't sway him. She wouldn't get off the hook so easy, and he wouldn't pass up the opportunity to get his hands on her bottom, either.

"You're an adult. You behaved impulsively, and now you'll accept your punishment like an adult."

He let the silence stretch out while she thought through her options—of which there were none as far as he was concerned. He'd wanted to get his hands on her ass ever since he walked in and saw her bending over the desk.

She would be a terrible poker player, he decided. Thoughts and emotions flitted across her face like messages on a digital billboard as she worked it all out in her impressive mind. She was physically beautiful, no doubt about it, but her incredible intellect was the biggest turn on of all. As a scientist, she understood the best discoveries came when a person kept an open mind. She might not know everything she liked or didn't like, but she would be willing to test any theory.

He gambled on her natural curiosity, and prayed she wouldn't turn him in for sexually blackmailing her—or worse. An assault charge would end his career faster than he could swat her butt.

One transparent thought at a time, she slowly came to the conclusion he knew she would.

"What do you want me to do?"

"Pull your shorts down then lay across my lap."

The pulse in her throat jumped, and the fingers he still held in his hand twitched. He rubbed his thumb over her knuckles. "You can still change your mind."

As he suspected, she took his comment as a challenge. She jerked her fingers free. He tried to keep his eyes on her face, but as soon as he heard the zipper slide down, nothing short of a blindfold would have kept him from looking.

"Panties, too."

She didn't argue, just worked her thumbs beneath the second layer of fabric and pushed. Inch by delicious inch, her creamy skin was revealed only to disappear as her T-shirt fell back into place. When her bare mound came into view, he almost went into cardiac arrest. He hadn't expected her perfect cleft to be so blatantly on display.

Before he could stop himself, he raised his hand to stop her shirt from dropping to cover her. Hands still on the waistband of her shorts, she froze.

"God, you're beautiful." He'd never meant anything so much in his life. A line of pink cleaved the slight mound of ivory flesh at the juncture of her thighs. He could only imagine how lovely her womanhood would be, flowered open to him. Already at attention, his dick jerked in protest at being denied access to her.

A slight tremble along her body brought him back to his senses. He wasn't going to fuck her. Not today. Not ever. He'd spank her, in part to indulge his need to touch her, and in part to remind them both their relationship had to remain professional.

"That's good." Her shorts were at mid-thigh. "Show me your ass." He patted his lap to indicate where he wanted her. After a heartbeat of hesitation, she draped herself across him, her hands going out to steady herself against the floor.

Placing his left hand between her shoulder blades to hold

her in place, he took a moment to enjoy the view. Her ponytail had fallen forward, exposing the graceful length of her neck leading to the knot at the top of her spine. Beneath his hand, her lungs filled and emptied at a steady rate. Fuck. She was calmer than he was.

"Have you ever done this before?"

"N-no. Have you?"

"Fuck, no." His gaze moved to her bottom. Her Mustangs T-shirt covered everything down to the twin creases pointing to forbidden territory. Willing his hand not to shake, he caressed her thigh then slowly inched his way up, taking the red fabric higher, exposing her perfect globes. Knowing he was making a huge mistake, he cupped her right cheek and squeezed. His dick jumped, and his balls tightened. Christ, he knew exactly how her body would feel as he slammed into her from behind, and his mind provided the imagery he would never see firsthand. Unable to stop himself, he massaged her left cheek, too.

His thighs felt like concrete beneath her ribs, but his hand on her bare backside—that was Heaven. If any of her academia associates saw her now, they'd never believe she'd willingly subjected herself to this. But, she'd do anything to preserve her research—even this. She'd wager many researchers had done worse things in the name of science.

When it came down to it, she'd made a huge mistake, and this was her punishment. Royce promised when it was over, he'd forget about what she'd done, and they could move forward again as researcher and research subject. As he palmed her cheeks, she tried not to think about how good his hand felt on her skin or how she longed for his fingers to explore down the crease he'd so far only brushed over.

Stop! Stop thinking about having sex with him! It isn't going to happen. He's made that perfectly clear. You crossed the line with your research subject. This is punishment. Punishment.

The first slap landed on her right cheek, sending every pain receptor in her brain into a panic. "Owwwww!" She tried to claw her way up, but Royce's big hand on her back refused to budge.

"Stay still."

"That hurt!" Tears clouded her vision.

"It's a spanking. Of course it hurt."

Another smack landed on her left cheek, and she doubled her efforts to escape. It didn't take long for her to figure out she was no match for his strength. No matter how much she wiggled, squirmed, or bucked, he held her down. Tears fell freely, and she had to wipe her snotty nose on her arm.

"Are you done?" God, how humiliating to be spanked like a child.

"Not by a long shot, babe." He'd secured her thighs with his arm. Since she'd quit trying to escape, he went back to stroking her ass, which felt like it was on fire. "I wish you could see this."

His touch was gentler than she could have imagined as he soothed her tender flesh. She sniffed to clear her nostrils and waited for…what? She knew what was coming next—he'd said he wasn't finished. Knowing didn't make the pain any less when his hand landed with unerring accuracy. After several swats, he stopped to caress her bottom. She sobbed so hard she couldn't understand a thing he said as his hand manipulated her bottom. At some point, his tender ministrations began to sink into her consciousness and she strained to hear his words.

"Beautiful. Fucking, beautiful."

"God, I need to touch you."

"Most beautiful thing I've ever seen."

His fingers traced the seam of her ass. "Want to touch you."

Her pussy throbbed at his words, and suddenly, she wanted him to touch her. Her bum hurt, but it was such a good hurt. She was wet, and the tissues between her legs were swollen, aching. When had that happened?

A single blunt digit delved into her crack, paused a heartbeat at her anus before continuing on toward her pussy.

She arched, offering him as much access as she could, given the state of her clothing. Why hadn't she pushed her shorts all the way to her ankles?

There was no time to beat herself up over her little oversight. His finger had found her valley. Groaning, he stroked through her sopping wet folds, rimming her vaginal entrance until she knew she was going to die unless he touched her *there*. Her clit throbbed with need. Just when she was certain he would ease her suffering, he withdrew his hand and, once again, peppered her bottom with solid blows.

She lost track of how many times he'd struck her. In mid-sob, she realized she'd begun aiding him at some point. Her hips worked in concert with his hand, begging him to strike her. Her head spun as she tried to rationalize what was happening to her. She no longer felt like a child being punished, she felt like a woman—aroused and desperate for release.

What would he think of her if she begged him to fuck her? God, she'd sunk low. From scientific researcher to shameless hussy in three days. It had to be some sort of record. But she was beyond caring about things like her reputation. Royce Stryker had destroyed her.

"Please." She wiggled, trying to draw her knees up so she could open her legs wider—anything to send the message she wanted to send. *Please, fuck me. Now.* Certain she'd only thought the words, she gasped when her tormentor shoved her shorts and panties down to her ankles. Before she could sigh in relief, he'd grabbed her around the waist and set her on her knees between his splayed legs.

"What?" Her body rebelled at the sudden loss of contact.

"Knees wide," he ordered. As she kicked one foot free of the fabric binding her, Royce yanked her T-shirt over her head, leaving her in nothing but a cotton bra. She looked up at him, wondering what he could possibly have in mind.

"You need to come."

She nodded, tears welling in her eyes, making it hard to see the expression on his face. She wanted to touch herself, to squeeze her legs tight around her fingers and find the sharp edge of release.

"Come here, then."

One big hand cradled the back of her head, bringing her forehead to his shoulder. "Put your hands on my thighs, and don't move them, no matter what."

Tricia gripped his legs, grateful for the steady rock beneath her forearms while her body quaked like a leaf in the wind.

"Take a deep breath." She inhaled. "Let it out." As the cleansing breath swooshed past her lips, a slap landed on her clit followed by another and another. Biting her bottom lip, she glanced down. Royce used his fingers like a paddle on the tender flesh between her legs. It was the single most erotic thing she'd ever seen.

Panting in tandem with the blows, she twisted the fabric of his trousers into her fists as the relentless pain took her up and up. Closer to the peak that seemed unattainable. She'd never come like this, from nothing but a spanking, didn't know if she could.

"Don't think about it, babe. Just let it come. I've got you."

God, did he have her. With nothing more than his palm cradling her head against his shoulder, he held her prisoner to her own need. Tricia closed her eyes and let herself feel every heated blow to her clit. *Slap! Slap! Slap!* Even the sound was erotic, evoking images of hot, sweaty bodies meeting in a frenzy.

Her labia took most of the abuse, but each strike sent shockwaves through her pussy. She smelled her own arousal, could feel the fluids coating her flesh, preparing her for penetration. Her vagina clenched, and she whimpered at the emptiness there.

Then she was coming, the muscles in her stomach tightening and releasing, setting off a chain reaction rocking her entire body.

She sobbed at the exquisite relief, the transcendent release tearing through her, turning her to putty in Royce's hands.

"There, there, sweet girl." With one hand, he petted her

head like he'd soothe a child with a skinned knee, but his other hand, the one that had wrought such damage to her body and her soul, stroked her pussy, easing the last jerky contractions with care as tender as his method of bringing her to orgasm had been brutal.

She took in a shuddering breath and let his big body support all of her weight. She didn't know when she'd be able to stand, much less look at the man who'd taken her apart, examined all her pieces, and reassembled her into a different person.

CHAPTER EIGHT

Damn. You are in deep shit, Stryker. Deep, deep, shit. He'd meant to teach Dr. Reed a lesson and appease his need to touch her, but his plans had turned to cinders the minute he gave in and touched her slick folds.

Spanking her had been a bad enough idea. But bringing her to orgasm was beyond bad. And holding her while she came apart—complete and utter insanity.

He'd never get her out of his head now that he knew the strangled sound she made in the back of her throat when she came, or the way her entire body seemed connected to her pleasure. God, and her scent. Roses on a hot summer day. He'd give anything to lay her back on the coffee table and taste her— to see if she was as sweet as her scent promised.

But he wouldn't do anything else with Dr. Reed. He'd already crossed a line professionally. And personally? Teetered on the edge of a cliff. He yanked himself back with sheer force of will. He couldn't let this thing with Tricia go any further.

Pushing her away, he grabbed her shirt from the floor and held it between them. He didn't even try to be civil for fear she'd read something into his tone that wasn't there. Could never be there. Not after the disaster he'd made of his marriage. Relationships were not his thing, and if he was reading the signposts correctly, another step and they'd be on Relationship Road. And there was no turning back once they made the leap. "We're even now. You can go."

He heard the shock hit her though she didn't move, didn't say a word. Hell, she was hardly breathing. Neither was he. Standing, he sucked in a deep breath and stepped away, leaving her on her knees facing an empty chair. He was being an ass, but there was no other choice. He needed to salvage his career, and from what he could tell, she didn't need personal involvement any more than he did. Calling it even today and ending whatever this was before it got any more complicated was the only solution.

With his hands fisted on his hips, he studied the ceiling while she righted her clothes. He'd seen most of her—enough to imprint her permanently on his brain. His imagination was perfectly capable of filling in the color and size of her nipples and the finer details of her pussy. At any rate, he had enough images filed away to fuel his fantasies for the rest of his life.

She scooted past him, headed back the way they'd come. He followed her, grabbing his keys up as they headed out the back door. When she got to her car, she opened the door then stopped. For the first time since he'd kicked her out of his house, she looked at him. Everything she felt was right there for the world to see—pain, humiliation, disbelief, anger, confusion. She had a right to every one of them.

"What are you doing?"

"I'm going to follow you home. Make sure you get there safely."

"You don't have to escort me. I'm fine." The tremor in her voice belied the confident tilt of her chin.

"It's the least I can do." Royce waited while she made up her mind—even though he had no intention of changing his. If she didn't want him to follow, he'd do it anyway, just from a more discreet distance. He might be a bastard, but he wouldn't sleep tonight until he knew she'd made it home and he was certain she wouldn't call once she was safe.

"Suit yourself." She climbed into the driver's seat and slammed the door hard enough to rattle his teeth.

You're an idiot. A complete idiot. Tricia blinked away tears as she navigated her way down Royce Stryker's driveway. A glance in the rearview mirror confirmed he was following her. Why he would want to, she had no idea. He'd more than made it clear they were done. Kaput. Over. *Fini.* Case closed.

He'd gotten even for what she'd done to him. A homerun on the first pitch. Out of the ballpark. Knocked the cover off the ball. Shattered her.

Her fingers tightened on the steering wheel. She probably owed him a new pair of slacks for what she'd done to the ones he was wearing. Her fingers still ached from holding on so tight. Add a new shirt to the mix. She'd cried all over his shoulder. No doubt there were makeup smears all over it, and that shit didn't come out.

"Screw you, Royce Stryker." She found a crumpled tissue in the console—a reminder she needed to clean out her car—and blew her nose. "You're rich. Buy your own fucking clothes. Serves you right."

Indignation felt good. Who was he to rock her world then push her away? *You're a jerk, Mr. Stryker.*

We're even. The words were a slap in the face. So childish when what they'd done was anything but.

He plays a game, A GAME, for a living. What else can you expect from him? Men in general are nothing but little boys playing games and that goes double with baseball players.

By the time she pulled into her reserved spot at her apartment complex, she'd convinced herself of her superiority, if not her adult status. As she put one foot on the ground, she was grateful her legs had ceased trembling at some point in the forty-five minute drive to her suburban neighborhood. Her place was nice as apartments went, but compared to Royce's home, it was a dump.

Some day in the next century or when she'd sold her system to every professional sports team and could afford it, she wanted a house of her own. Nothing as grand as the one she'd just left, but a few rooms with hardwood floors, big windows, and a yard where she could plant stuff.

Royce probably had a team of gardeners armed with sharp tools to keep anyone from touching a single leaf. The kind of casual elegance surrounding his house didn't just happen on its own.

Shaking off the memory of the peace she'd sensed when she had followed him past the ominous gates guarding his property, she headed for her door. Up the stairs, second door on the left. Her windows looked out on the small green space between buildings instead of the parking lot. Every step she took, she was aware of his gaze following her. His expensive sports car purred like a kitten at the curb. Yet another thing to make her hate him. She could buy a house with acreage for what he'd probably paid for his car.

Thank God, Royce couldn't see her hand shake as she slid her key into the lock. Distance and poor exterior illumination insured that.

Once inside, she closed and locked the door. Her legs carried her as far as the sofa where she collapsed. Dragging her knees up, she hugged her legs to her chest to stop the trembling she couldn't seem to control. Her position pulled her shorts tight in the crotch, so after a few minutes she had to stretch out to relieve the ache between her legs.

She never would have gone to his house if she'd known what he had in mind. Hell, he was entitled to his revenge, but had it been necessary to take it in a way she would never be able to forget it? Forget him? Her ass hurt from the spanking, and her pussy throbbed as if his hand continued to slap the tender tissues. She'd never dreamed she could enjoy something like what he'd done to her, but God, she had.

If she closed her eyes, she could see his long, cotton-clad arm between them. A perfectly starched cuff circling his wrist—his palm and fingers forming a paddle he applied with expert skill to her pussy. Over and over until she came so hard she cried out. And she'd do it all again, anytime, anywhere. If he'd only ask.

That's how far gone she was.

Grabbing a throw pillow, she held it to her face and screamed until her vocal chords protested. Then she gave in and cried like a baby.

Tricia arrived at the stadium early, half expecting security to turn her away or, at the very least, escort her to the General Manager's office where she'd be told to pack her things and leave. When her key still turned the lock on her temporary office, she breathed a sigh of relief.

Royce wouldn't pitch today. The Mustangs used a five game rotation for their starting pitchers, so he wouldn't pitch again until the second game of their next road trip. He would do a light workout, and she would monitor as much as possible via the wireless connections. The rest of her time would be spent analyzing the data she'd already collected and recording her thoughts and observations thus far. If there were lapses in the data, she'd work on fixing the problems before Stryker took to the mound again.

After checking to make sure the equipment needed for today was in working order, she opened her laptop and powered up the software program that had cost her every penny she could beg, borrow, or save.

Referring back to her notes, she noted the activity Royce had engaged in at each time stamp. It took some doing, but after saving the incriminating data to a separate, password-protected file, she deleted the evidence of what she'd done. If her research ever amounted to anything, she'd have to account for the gap in the recording. Perhaps she could chalk it up to an equipment malfunction. This early in the project, the excuse would be believable.

She thought she was prepared to see him, to play it cool

as if she hadn't done what she'd done, and he hadn't split her like an atom. But when he walked in wearing a suit and tie and looking like several million bucks and an ice cream sundae, her body flushed and her mouth watered. The *swoosh* of air following him in carried a hint of expensive cologne and a special note that was uniquely Royce Stryker.

When she looked up and saw him standing in the doorway, her pussy clenched. She shifted in her seat, the movement reminding her of the tender spots on her ass where he'd spanked her the night before. A night spent bolstering her confidence had proved more useless than an eight-inch floppy disc as every ounce of resolve she'd cobbled together crumbled to ash. She'd do anything he wanted. Right here. Right now. Project be damned.

"Just thought I'd let you know I'm here. I'll go change. No batting practice for me today, just some light throwing to keep the arm loose, but it can wait until we're done in here."

She nodded, not trusting her voice.

"Shorts?"

She nodded again.

"Okay, then. I'll see you in a few."

Okay. She stared at the closed door, willing her brain to catch up to reality. He'd said everything would be forgotten after her punishment, and apparently it had been as far as he was concerned. *Easy for him to move on as if nothing happened. His ass isn't sore today.*

He'd seemed perfectly at ease with her while she'd become a horny mute the second she saw him. Tricia stood so she could pace and think. Her bottom instantly felt better, but the freedom of movement did nothing to help blood flow to her brain. *Too bad you can't scrub your brain the way you can a hard drive.* The images stored in her gray matter were there to stay, there to torment her with what she couldn't have.

It was time to put on her big girl panties and act like the professional she claimed to be.

CHAPTER NINE

Good. She's here. Royce let the door close behind him and headed for the locker room. After the way he'd treated Tricia the previous evening, he hadn't been at all sure she would show up today. And if she did, there was a good chance she would go straight to management and file sexual harassment charges against him.

Royce changed into a pair of shorts, but since he wasn't scheduled to pitch, he wore briefs underneath instead of a jock strap. The difference between the two was all in his head. If he *believed* there was more fabric between him and Tricia, then there was.

He'd need every trick in the book to get through an afternoon with her and not touch her. Spanking her was supposed to cleanse her from his system. His promise of forgive and forget had been a load of bullshit. He'd never forgive her for barreling into his life and turning it upside down, and there was no way in hell he would forget the way her mouth had felt on him or the way she'd looked—on her knees while she sucked him off.

Shit. He'd never thought of himself as particularly dominant, but when it came to the lovely Dr. Reed, his mind traveled a different road, one with kinks and switchbacks enough to make him dizzy with need.

Spanking had never been his thing, but sweet Heaven, his hand itched to have another go at her ass. He flexed his fingers then rubbed his damp palm on his shorts. Seeing his handprint on her ivory skin had tripped a switch inside him—the fucking-insane-with-need switch. Then, when he'd realized how turned on the good doctor had become, the insanity just kept coming. It had taken every ounce of self-control he had to keep from burying his cock deep inside her and fucking her until they both couldn't walk.

Instead, he'd spanked her clit until she flew apart at his feet. Fuckin' insanity.

He'd been so turned on and so disgusted with his lack of control, he'd acted like a bastard, practically ordering her out of his house without so much as a thank you for the way she'd trusted him with her body. Her trust had been misplaced, but she'd given it all the same. And he'd taken full advantage. He hadn't even been aware a woman could come that way, but after the first few slaps, he'd abandoned his original plan to finger fuck her and kept up the onslaught on her clit.

Her response had destroyed him. Fuckin' tore him up inside.

Thank God he'd remembered who she was—who *he* was—in time to put an end to the evening before he'd done more damage. He knew calling them even had made him sound like a jerk, but he was a man who kept score. They were tied, one orgasm to one orgasm. Game over. They weren't going extra innings. No more games.

He'd called on the last bit of gentleman inside him to make sure she got home safely then he returned home and tried to wipe the previous hours from his brain. She'd spent less than an hour in his house, but everywhere he went, she was present. All he had to do was close his eyes to see her in his kitchen, his den, his bedroom. Even when he stood in the center of his empty living room, he saw her standing next to the fireplace, a glass of champagne in her hand, and a gleam in her eyes to outshine her form-fitting evening gown.

Where the image came from, he had no idea. All he'd seen her in was shorts and T-shirts, and he'd seen her wearing nothing but a bra. Still, he knew, without a doubt, she would look fantastic in evening wear. And he'd like nothing more than to help her remove it so he could kiss every inch of exposed skin. He'd start at her shoulders and work his way down to her toes. Then he'd do it all again in reverse order, drinking in the scent of summer roses as he went.

When he opened the door, she'd turned to face him. Involuntarily, his gaze swept her from head to toe. She looked okay. Better than okay. Fucking fabulous. Knowing what was underneath her simple attire, his mind did the conversion automatically. His mouth watered remembering the scent of her arousal on his fingers.

He forced his eyes up to her face. Her gaze was steady, but her bottom lip trembled. He swept his gaze over her body again, this time taking note of the important things. She was shaking like a leaf in a mulching machine waiting for the blades to chew it up.

He sobered quickly. Was she afraid of him?

"I'm sorry."

"I'm sorry."

Their words trampled over each other.

Royce was afraid to move, but every cell in his body screamed for him to go to her, to assure her no one would ever hurt her, least of all him. But he had hurt her. Physically and perhaps on a deeper level. He turned, reaching for the door handle. "I'll go."

"No!"

He looked over his shoulder.

The fingers of one hand covered her mouth as if to keep more words from spilling out. Then, miraculously, they did. "Don't go."

It took supreme effort to pry his fingers loose then turned

back to her. "I'm sorry about last night. I had no right to touch you the way I did." She'd been staring at him, wide-eyed, but at the mention of his inappropriate behavior, she cast her gaze to the floor. And if he wasn't mistaken, a blush was creeping from the V-neck of her shirt all the way to her cheeks. "I thought you would have gone to management by now. You have every right to."

"I couldn't."

"Why not? I promise I won't try to discredit you in any way. However much you want to tell them, I'll go along with."

The fingers on her right hand toyed with the pencils in a cup on the corner of her desk. Her breasts rose and fell as she took a deep breath. Then she lifted her chin and looked at him.

"I won't do it for two reasons. One, because they'd put an end to my research. I can't let that happen."

He nodded. She'd obviously put a lot of time, effort, and money into her project. Pulling the plug on it at this phase, and for those reasons, would kill it completely. The same way telling would kill his career. But he'd done the deed. He was man enough to accept what was coming to him. Hell, his career was on life support anyway.

"And the second reason?"

"Because I liked what we did."

Royce stared at her. He'd wrestled his body under control, but his brain was malfunctioning. It had to be. She could not possibly have said what he thought she did. "What?"

"I said...I liked what we did. I know we can't do it again, but—"

"The hell we can't." One of his brains was functioning, and that was enough. He slid the deadbolt home, ensuring no one would walk in on them, then grabbed her hand. Dragging her into the far corner where no one peering through the narrow window in the door could see them, he backed her up against the wall.

Pinning her wrists beside her head, he bent so they were face-to-face. She was breathing hard, and when her tongue swept across her bottom lip, he couldn't squelch the groan rising from his throat. "You make me crazy when you do that."

"Do what?"

"Breathe." He covered her mouth with his, sliding his tongue along the seam until she opened, letting him inside. She tasted of coffee and sugar, and like a caffeine addict, he couldn't get enough.

Dropping her wrists, he brought her hips up against his with one hand while the other angled her head so he could go deeper. A low moan rattling from her throat, she wrapped her arms around his shoulders as if she were drowning and only he could save her.

He thought he might die when she thrust her tongue between his lips, taking what she needed with bold strokes. Her fingers playing through the hair at his nape were his undoing. He wanted her. Here. Now. His career be damned.

Definitely the smaller of his two brains making the decision, but hormones overrode common sense. He slid his hand between them, feeling like a blind man, and worked his way underneath the hem of her shirt to the waistband of her shorts. The button and zipper were no match for his determined fingers. In moments, he was stroking into her wet heat with one finger, then two.

He broke the kiss, held her head so they were cheek-to-cheek. He inhaled deeply, taking in the musk of her arousal combined with the sweet rose scent he would forever associate with her. "God, sweetheart," he breathed against her ear. "You are so fuckin' wet."

"I want to feel you, too." Before he could stop her, she dropped one hand between them. Finding his straining erection, she measured his length and girth, stroking him through the layers of his clothing. It wasn't enough. Not even close.

"Push my shorts down. I need to feel your hand on me."

He forgot all about how wonderful her fingers felt in his hair when having shoved his shorts and boxers down, she wrapped her free hand around his aching dick.

"Fuck, that feels good." Her touch was untutored,

sometimes light, sometimes tight enough to restrict blood flow, but he had no intention of stopping her explorations. When his release came, it would be all the sweeter for the little bit of pain endured along the way.

"You're big." Her breath fanned over his earlobe, sending shivers down his spine. "I could barely take you in my mouth."

Mention of the blow job she'd given him in the supply closet made his dick jerk with renewed enthusiasm. He'd never forget the ecstasy of her hot, wet mouth surrounding him. It would go down as one of his all-time fondest memories. "Next time I'm inside you, I'm going to be in here." He fingered her pussy in a not so subtle imitation of what he'd like to do with his cock. Her hand tightened on him like a rookie in his first at-bat. Much more and he would come all over both of them.

"Easy," he said, trapping her and his cock with his free hand. When she stilled, he moved to her shorts. "Help me get these off you."

She did all the work while he held his dick out of the way, only letting go when he could press it up against her soft belly.

"That's better. Hold on, babe. I'm going to make you come."

The short top she'd worn today flared out at her hips, leaving her exposed. Tricia gripped Royce's hips to steady herself. She drew him into her lungs with every labored breath she took. Beneath her palms, his skin was smooth and hot, his body chiseled granite. A bead of pre-cum cooled on her stomach where his cock rubbed against her.

Flesh, tender from the previous evenings activities, magnified the ache of arousal between her legs. No matter how much she'd tried to convince herself otherwise, she wanted— needed—Royce's touch.

"Please."

"Shh, babe. I'm gonna take care of you." He pressed his lips to her temple then to her cheek. No one had ever sworn to take care of her so passionately. Desire shuddered through her body. He worked his way down, leaving wet kisses along her skin then nuzzling her through the thin fabric of her shirt and bra. Her nipples, already tight, strained to get closer.

His hands came to rest on her hips, then ever so slowly, inched beneath her shirt, learning her shape one rib at a time until his palms closed over her aching mounds. She moaned and melted into his hands.

"So soft." He squeezed and massaged while his lips continued their downward trek. When he pushed beneath her top and dipped his tongue into her navel, she came up on her tiptoes and curled her fingers into his hair. She tugged with all the strength she could muster, but he wouldn't be budged.

"Babe." His breath raised goose flesh on her stomach. "I need to taste you." He dragged the tip of his nose along her cleft as if to emphasize his point. "Open for me."

Before she could form an answer, yes or no, he had one of her legs draped over his shoulder. A hysterical laugh caught in her throat. No one, not even her gynecologist had ever examined her as closely as the man kneeling between her legs. She could feel his heated gaze on her, and it was enough to stir the well of arousal low in her belly.

"So fuckin' beautiful."

The first swipe of his tongue almost toppled her. Royce didn't miss a beat. Continuing his intimate exploration, he raised one arm, trapping her thigh atop his shoulder while his hand pressed against her abdomen, pinning her against the wall.

His mouth was magic. His tongue flicked over her clit then delved lower, rimming her entrance then thrusting inside her in a kiss any Frenchman would be proud of. She flexed her hips, opening herself more fully to him. He didn't disappoint. He moved his mouth over her inner lips, stroking and sucking, bringing all her nerve endings alive in a way that was entirely different from his attentions the previous night, but achieved the same mind-blowing effect. A familiar tension took hold of her insides, tightening with every lick, every suck, every scrape of his teeth. She climbed toward the peak, her head thrashing back and forth as she struggled to contain the cries of pleasure threatening to escape.

A tiny voice in the back of her head warned her of the folly of her actions, but like every time she was anywhere near Royce Stryker, reason sat on the bench.

Hands flat against the wall, Tricia braced herself for the inevitable fall from the cliff. One more lick. One more nip at her clit.

Her body convulsed while Royce's mouth coaxed every last drop from her. Wrung out and weeping from the effort it took to keep from screaming his name, she collapsed into his arms. Holding her close, he turned them and slid down to sit on the floor with his back against the wall. Tricia curled into his lap like a weak kitten, unable to do anything but whimper and cry.

What had he done to her? She wasn't the kind of woman who fell apart because of an orgasm. But with him? Falling apart seemed to be the norm.

He held her head against his shoulder with one hand while the other skimmed over her lower body. When his fingers dipped between her thighs, she willingly gave him access. "I've never seen anything so beautiful in my life."

Between being spanked to orgasm the previous night and what they'd just done, her pussy was beyond tender, yet with a few gentle strokes, arousal began to build again. She wiggled her bare butt. He'd somehow managed to pull his shorts back up. When, she had no idea. Turning her face into his shoulder, she groaned and opened herself wider. Were there no limits to her depravity?

Apparently not.

Sitting in his lap, half dressed while he patiently worked her toward yet another orgasm seemed like the most rational thing she'd ever done.

He hadn't meant to get her all worked up again, at least not so soon. He'd only wanted to touch her, to help ease the tenderness he'd caused, but the second she opened for him, he realized she needed more than just comfort.

Whatever you need, babe. I'll give it to you.

Outside their door, he heard the normal level of activity to be expected this close to game time. Someone would come looking for him eventually, but until they did, there was nowhere he'd rather be than sitting on the cold floor fingering Tricia to orgasm as many times as she needed.

She curled into him, and as her climax neared, her hands clenched into fists pulling his shirt tight. His shoulder muffled the gasps and moans issuing from her lips as pleasure tightened its grip. He held her while he crooned encouraging words into her hair. She was so damn sweet and trusting. Not to mention, responsive. He and Hannah had been together for a long time, and sex had been a healthy part of their relationship right up to the very end, but Royce couldn't remember a time when his ex had given herself to him without reservation the way Tricia had every time they'd been together.

When Tricia was no longer a part of his life, he'd treasure these moments spent with her. Until then, he was going to make sure she never forgot either.

"That's it, sweetheart. Let it come."

He slid his fingers in…out…back in, all the while he used the heel of his hand on her clit. Every breath he took brought her scent into his lungs where, like most of his blood, it went straight to his dick. His balls were going to explode, but he was willing to make the sacrifice. For reasons he didn't want to contemplate, Tricia's pleasure had become more important than his own.

She was so close. The walls of her vagina clamped down tight enough to cut off the circulation in his fingers. He managed to curl his fingertips up, found the hidden secret, and tapped. Once. Twice.

Her orgasm was a thing of beauty, breaking over her like a summer storm—fast, violent, and in the end, peaceful. He cupped her pussy, capturing the flood of her desire in his palm while holding her close until her fingers eased their grip on his shirt and she spit out the wad of cotton knit she'd clenched between her teeth during her climax. His T-shirt was most likely a done for, but he couldn't regret the loss. It had given its life in a good cause. He chuckled at the thought.

"What are you laughing about?" Her voice sounded weak as a newborn kitten, but there was a trace of backbone to the tone hinting at the fierce cat on the horizon. Tricia was stronger than she appeared on the outside. He liked that about her.

"My shirt. Is there anything left of it?"

She smoothed the abused material with one small hand. "I'm sorry. I didn't mean to ruin your clothes."

"No worries." He covered her hand with his. "It's a good thing you don't have me wired up. Your computer would probably be dialing 9-1-1 right about now."

"Your pulse is racing." The concern in her voice made his runaway heart swell almost to bursting.

"Yeah, well, making you come is exhilarating, to say the least." He used their clasped hands to tilt her chin up so he could brush his lips against hers. "I feel like I just ran a marathon, but instead of being tired, I'm ready to go again."

When she tugged her hand free and wrapped it around his nape, he kissed her again. Slanting his mouth over hers, he held nothing back. He poured every ounce of his desire into the kiss, drawing her lower lip between his teeth, thrusting his tongue deep inside to taste the uniqueness that was her.

Someone tugged on the locked door, startling them apart. *Thump! Thump! Thump!* "Yo! Strikeout. You in there?"

Royce recognized the voice. Antonio Ramirez, the Mustangs' center fielder. What the fuck could he want, and how did he know to find him here?

Tricia tried to scramble off his lap, but Royce held her easily with one arm around her waist. "Shh," he whispered in her ear. "He'll go away." The last thing they needed was for her to accidentally move into the line of sight the narrow vertical window in the door allowed. Better to pretend they weren't there until she had her clothes back on and his erection abated. Tricia ceased her attempts to stand, but her posture was anything but relaxed.

Royce cupped her jaw, turning her face to him. He saw fear and something else, embarrassment, perhaps, in her eyes. She had to be feeling vulnerable, sitting across his lap in nothing more than a thin T-shirt while he was still fully dressed. He brought his mouth to her ear. "Don't move a muscle. Don't make a sound."

Easing back, he looked into her eyes. She bit her lower lip and nodded.

Releasing her, he sat up straight, reached over his shoulder, grabbed the back of his shirt and yanked it over his head. Leaning back against the wall, he draped the knit fabric over her lap, covering her just in case someone managed to find a key to the room. Instantly, Tricia relaxed in his arms. She buried her face in the crook of his neck. Her breath seared his skin then she touched her lips to a spot behind his ear lobe. The tiny kiss of thanks unraveled what was left of his resolve to leave her alone.

CHAPTER TEN

Calling a halt before he went another round with Tricia left him agitated, not to mention frustrated, but they had no choice. They'd taken too many chances at the stadium all ready. Hell, anyone with a key could have walked in on them earlier, and the idea of anyone else seeing Tricia in a compromising position made his blood boil. *Not gonna happen.* The next time he got her naked, she'd be in his bed, and they weren't going to stop with what amounted to glorified making out. As far as he was concerned, she was his, but he needed to stake his claim by fucking her until neither one of them could stand.

"Meet me after the game. We'll go to my place."

She held on to his arm while she stepped into her panties. Hannah had never worn plain white cotton panties, not even when they'd been in high school. He'd teased her about the inexpensive garments with cartoon characters or suggestive words printed on them, so when he began making money, she'd switched to expensive lace and satin. He was never sure if she made the switch to end the teasing or if she really thought the fancy stuff was more attractive. If she'd bothered to ask him, he would have told her to go back to the discount store. But she never asked, and he never spoke up.

"Nice panties."

Tricia's face flamed. She grabbed her shorts out of his hands and stepped into them quickly. "I wasn't expecting anyone to see them."

"Come here." He wrapped one arm around her waist, pulling her close. With his free hand, he released the button and zipper on her shorts. "I wasn't making fun of you. I really like your choice of undergarments." His fingers stroked the soft fabric covering her stomach. "I know you weren't trying to seduce me or anyone else, but trust me, these are sexy. I'm going to have a bat in my pants all night thinking about taking these off of you later."

He refastened her shorts and stepped away. "Meet me after the game?" He repeated his earlier words, asking this time instead of demanding. Grabbing his shirt off the floor, he pulled it over his head. Every second he waited for her answer seemed like a lifetime.

"Okay."

Relief washed over him. He smiled and drew her back into his arms for a quick kiss. "Just so you know. I'm going to take you to bed tonight, Dr. Reed. I'm going to peel those sexy panties off and fuck you all night long. If you aren't on the same page, then go home now."

He didn't wait for her answer. Couldn't bear to hear her say she'd changed her mind and wouldn't be there to meet him tonight. He'd deal with the possibility she didn't want him the way he wanted her when the time came.

"You lookin' for me?" Royce caught up with Tony in the locker room.

"Yeah, man. Doyle said you were working with some researcher or something. He wasn't too clear, but I gather I'm supposed to be her next test subject. He said you would introduce me and fill me in on the program."

Images of Tricia's hands on Tony flashed through Royce's brain. *Fuck.* Somewhere in the back of his mind, he'd known more subjects would be needed for her research, but for whatever reason, he'd never considered they would be his teammates. *Holy hell.*

"She's not ready to take on anyone else yet." He had no idea if the statement was true or not, but he'd be damned if she was going to put her hands on another man, especially Tony Ramirez. The center fielder was married to the stadium organist, but it was no secret he was once a member of Bases Loaded, a secret sex club within the league. "I'll let you know when that changes." *Don't hold your breath, buddy.*

"Hey, no problem. I'm not sure I want to be some scientist's lab rat, but Doyle said this was something the League wanted to see completed." He shrugged. "Guess I'll see it through, though I'm not happy about it."

"Me either, but I was hardly in a position to say no. Management is hoping for a miracle cure for my inability to throw strikes."

Tony smirked. "Sex, man. Lots of sex. It's the answer to everything."

"You aren't the first person to suggest I get laid. I wish it was that simple."

"Won't know until you try."

Was it *that* obvious he wasn't getting any since his divorce? "Yeah, well. I loved Hannah." Royce raked a hand through his hair. Tricia's scent on his fingers caught in his lungs. Damn. He couldn't keep using his divorce as an excuse for his poor pitching. Not when he'd had his fingers knuckle deep inside another woman moments ago.

"She's gone, dude. Get over it."

"I hear you." A headache was brewing at the base of his neck. He rubbed the tense muscles. "Thanks for the advice, however stupid it was."

Tony smiled. "Not stupid if it's true."

Unwilling to confirm or deny his sex stats, Royce turned.

"Since I'm not pitching today, I think I'll go see if I can get a massage before the game. I feel a headache coming on."

He was halfway to the door when Tony called out. "See if you can get laid, instead."

Without stopping, Royce waved a hand to acknowledge his teammate's sage advice.

Get laid. He planned to do that all right, but he wasn't going to tell Tony or anyone else.

Tricia stared at the computer screen. Numbers, graph lines and lines of data blurred together into a meaningless jumble even Einstein couldn't decipher. Somewhere in there was something significant. She could feel it in her bones, but what it was completely eluded her. All her brain seemed capable of focusing on at the moment was tonight. Was she really going to meet Royce after the game? For sex?

He hadn't minced words. *I'm going to fuck you all night long.*

Holy, smoley. Even after two orgasms, his softly spoken promise made her ache. She'd thought he would find out what Tony wanted and come back so she could wire him up and get more data, but she hadn't seen or heard from him since he all but ordered her to come to his bed tonight.

She wasn't inclined to say no. She'd never felt the kind of things Royce made her feel. And, he'd said he liked the serviceable white cotton panties she'd worn today. Tricia shook her head, and a giggle escaped her lips. She'd chosen the plain cotton ones because there was nothing more uncomfortable than sweating in lace or nylon, not to mention, the idea of scratchy fabric rubbing against her aching pubis all day long was unbearable.

Remembering her other reason for wearing nondescript panties brought to mind the previous evening, and the way it had ended. *We're even.*

All the feelings she'd experienced when he uttered those crushing words came flooding back, drowning her desire under a tidal wave of disgust and humiliation. She should have learned her lesson last night. She'd come to the stadium today prepared to be professional, to put everything they'd done together behind her. Instead, she'd confessed the one thing she never should have told anyone, let alone, Royce Stryker.

How stupid can you be? Telling him you liked the…the spanking? Stupid. Stupid. Stupid.

Thanks to her stupidity, she had plenty more to add to her list of things she never should have done. Still, she couldn't find it in herself to regret a single thing she'd done with Royce. He'd given her more pleasure in two days than she'd had in all the years since she lost her virginity combined.

Regrets? No. He'd shown her what passion was, and a part of her would always be grateful to him for opening her eyes to what she could have with the right person. No doubt she would learn even more in his bed, but those weren't the kind of things she was here to learn.

We're even.

Not by a long shot, Mr. Stryker. In a way, she'd always be in his debt, but he was a man who liked to keep score, so it was time to tie the game.

Tricia powered down her computer, stuffing it and the stack of reports she'd printed off into her canvas messenger bag. She sang along to the national anthem as she traversed the empty hallways of the Mustangs' underground facility.

A short time later, she drove out of the parking lot. "Now, we're even."

She wasn't waiting for him. Royce backtracked to her office. The light was off, and the door locked. He knocked and called her name, just in case she was in there, though why she would be sitting in the dark, he couldn't imagine. He considered calling her, but then he remembered he didn't have her phone number.

You know where she lives.

On the drive to her apartment, he came up with every reason he could think of for her to have left early. The one he didn't want to contemplate, however, refused to go away.

She doesn't want you to fuck her.

If there had been any other reason, she would have left a message for him. A woman as organized as she was wouldn't leave without a word, unless leaving *was* the word.

Royce pulled into Tricia's apartment complex. Her car was parked in the same slot she'd used the previous night when he'd kicked her out of his house then followed her home. He put the transmission in Park then opened his door. With one foot on the ground and the other on the car's floorboard, he gazed up at the dark landing leading to Tricia's door.

He was still trying to decide if he should go up and talk to her when a car pulled up behind his. A flash of bright headlights indicated the impatient driver wanted him to move his car.

"Fuck." Royce slid back into the driver's seat and sped out of the parking lot.

He had a splitting headache no amount of painkiller would alleviate. His mind knew he wasn't going to fuck Tricia anytime soon, but his body had a harder time dealing with the news. After a restless night where he woke repeatedly with a hard-on that refused to go away, he'd jerked off in the shower in a desperate attempt to find some relief.

The woman had a lot to answer for. Apparently, her first paddling hadn't been enough. He'd bend her over his knee again, give her the spanking she deserved. Then he'd fuck her senseless.

The door to her office stood open. Her melodic voice, carrying down the hard surfaces of the hallway, went straight to his groin, negating what little peace he'd found earlier beneath the rushing water.

Another voice, deep and decidedly male, unleashed

something primal and dangerous inside him. He'd kill anyone who touched her. Tricia was his.

Ready to pummel whoever dared touch his woman, Royce stepped into the room and came to an abrupt halt.

"Strikeout. Glad you could make it."

"Doyle." Royce glanced from the team manager to Tricia then back again. "What's up?"

"Just checking in to see how things are going. Dr. Reed says everything is going smoothly, but she's anxious to get more game-day data."

"I pitch on a five-game rotation."

"We've discussed your schedule. She's aware of the time constraints. That's why we've agreed to give her another test subject to work with in between your pitching dates."

Royce's blood boiled. "Tony?"

Doyle nodded. "Ramirez. Yeah, he should be here in a few minutes. If he gives you any trouble, let me know. His wife is my niece. I'll call her, and she'll set him straight. Clare has him wrapped around her little finger."

Royce had seen the couple a few times, and he silently agreed with Doyle. Tony Ramirez was pussy-whipped. Had been ever since he first laid eyes on Clare. "I'll make sure he behaves himself. No need to call the lady with the whips."

Doyle held up a hand. "Please. If they're into that sort of thing, I. Do. Not. Want to know about it."

"Just a figure of speech," Royce assured with a chuckle. He hadn't heard any rumors in that direction, but he'd been at the Crystal Ball last year when Doyle's niece arrived in the company of her then fiancé, Tony Ramirez, and three other baseball players from various teams. From the looks the men gave the future Mrs. Ramirez, she'd charmed their pants off. Literally. He wasn't going to voice his suspicions to the woman's uncle though. Royce valued his life too much.

"I'm sure he'll behave himself. If he doesn't, I'll threaten to shock him with an electrode." Tricia held up the business end of one of her wires. "That should keep him in line."

"You told me those things don't shock."

For the first time since he'd entered the room, she looked his way. "Did I say that?"

Royce had to make a physical effort to keep his jaw from dropping to the floor.

Doyle laughed. "Seems like you have everything under control. We'll talk soon, Royce."

He waited until the manager's footsteps trailed off down the hall. Then he exploded. "Are you fuckin' kidding me?" He pointed a shaky finger at the cord she still held aloft. "Those things could shock me?"

Tricia dropped the wire before collapsing into her chair behind the desk. "No, you idiot. They won't shock you." She shook her head. "Do you think I'd lie to you?"

"You did yesterday." His near-sleepless night, coupled with the real possibility of her putting her hands on fuckin' Tony Ramirez had darkened his mood from annoyed to pissed off. And she didn't even have the good sense to appear contrite.

"After you left, I changed my mind. You did say if I didn't want to take you up on your *generous* offer I should go home." She shrugged and reached for a stack of papers on her desk. "So I did."

He glared at her while she calmly stacked and shuffled papers, ignoring him. Finally, she stopped and looked up at him with eyes as hard as steel. "I think we're even now."

Even. The word echoed through his skull, joining the hammering behind his eyes from the headache from hell. So, that's what this was about—getting even. "Okay." He held his hands up chest high in mock surrender. "You got me there. I treated you badly the other night, and you got me back. Fair is fair."

"Fair is you leaving me alone to do my job." Moisture dammed along her lower eyelids, looking like it could spill over at any moment. He felt like an ass. Thinking about nothing but sex when he should be considering the whole thing from her point of view. His career was his business. He had no right to bring hers down.

"I'm sorry, Tricia. You're absolutely right." He straightened and backed away from her desk, giving her space. "I'm not going to lie and tell you I don't want you, but I promise I won't pressure you for anything more than you're willing to give. You need a test subject, I'm here for you. My body is yours."

He watched helplessly as she dug in her giant carry-all and came up with a tissue she used to dab at her eyes. He would have given her his shirt if he'd thought she would have taken it from him.

"I know I started all this with my inappropriate behavior, and I apologize." She sniffed back tears then squared her shoulders like a warrior ready for battle. "Since I started it, it's my place to end it."

God, he wanted her. And not because of the sex. Well, sex wasn't the only reason. He admired her backbone. It had taken nearly a decade for Hannah to find the words to tell him what she wanted, needed out of life. Until then, she'd gone along with everything that happened in his life as if she didn't have any goals of her own. And he'd let her.

It had been so much easier to believe his wife was happy than to deal with the possibility that she wasn't. He and Hannah both were to blame for the way their marriage turned out. He understood his self-centered attitude hadn't fostered an open atmosphere for communication, except in bed. Even Hannah would vouch for his attentiveness in bed. But sex hadn't been enough to hold the marriage together.

Royce nodded. "I appreciate your honesty, though I could have made you stop. Full disclosure here. I didn't want you to stop. I enjoyed every second your mouth was on me, and I look forward to the end of the month when I'm no longer your test subject."

Her gaze was direct, clinically assessing. "Why?"

"Because I intend to pick up where we left off."

He watched the muscles work in her throat as she swallowed hard, her gaze darting to the spot in the corner of the room where he'd made her come—twice. He might be clueless about some things, but desire in a woman's eyes wasn't one of them. She was as affected by what they'd done yesterday as he was.

"Believe it or not, I respect your research. My actions indicate otherwise, but from now on, you can count on me. I promise." Before she could respond, a knock sounded on the door. Tricia leaned to the side in order to see around him. Royce half turned to look over his shoulder.

"Looks like I'm in the right place." Tony Ramirez entered the room, an uncertain smile on his face.

"Hi." Tricia stepped from behind the desk, her arm outstretched and a huge smile on her face. "I'm Dr. Reed, but you can call me Tricia."

Tony took her hand for a brief handshake. "Antonio Ramirez. Everybody calls me Tony. Except my wife. Clare calls me Antonio."

Perfect. He's nervous. Royce figured it wouldn't take much to scare the big guy off. He smiled at his teammate. "Glad you could make it." The two shook hands.

"Care to tell me what this is all about?" The center fielder's gaze darted around the room as if looking for the hidden dangers.

"Dr. Reed is going to hook you up to her computer and run a bunch of tests on you." He clapped Tony on the back. "Nothing to worry about. It doesn't hurt much."

The big man's face turned white and his eyes nearly popped out of his head. It was all Royce could do to contain his laughter. His friend took a step backward—toward the door. "Look. Maybe I'm not the right person for this."

"Stop it, Royce." Tricia glared at him for a second before turning her attention to her next victim. "Tony, I promise I'm not going to hurt you. Mr. Stryker was just kidding." Her gaze swung back to him. The banked fury in her eyes confirmed his own thoughts.

You're being an ass again. The idea of her putting her hands on any other man, much less the one inching his way to the door, made him crazy, but he'd be the biggest jackass in the world to interfere with her work. He grabbed Tony by the arm and dragged him to the center of the room. "She isn't going to hurt you, but I suggest you do some serious shaving before you let her put those electrode patch things on you. I didn't, and I cried like a baby when she ripped them off."

From the stricken expression on the other man's face, Royce wasn't doing a very good job of convincing him he was going to be fine. "Shaving? You mean besides my face?"

"Yep. Chest, arms, legs. If your underwear covers it then it's okay. The rest?" He ran his hand over his hairless forearm. "Smooth is the new look."

"Seriously?" A big grin broke across his face. "Clare is going to *love* this." He rubbed his hands together like a kid who'd just been told he could have anything in the candy store he wanted. "When do we start?"

Royce rolled his eyes. Tricia smiled. "Mr. Stryker is right. The less hair, the less pain, but body hair doesn't interfere with my readings. It's up to you. If you want to do some hair removal at home, then we'll just do the preliminary stuff today."

Tony's expression grew serious. "Prelims it is. What's first?"

"First is a blood test."

Royce smirked as Tony's naturally dark skin paled.

The following day, Royce was finishing up another round of *wired* exercises when Tricia's new test subject arrived. Though he was free to go, he hung around the small office. Happily married or not, he still wasn't comfortable leaving Tricia alone with Ramirez, especially knowing how her hands felt pressing the electrode pads to the man's skin. Tony would have to be a monk not to respond, and when he did, Royce was going to pound him into the ground.

Tricia yanked the pads off Royce's back while he tugged

the ones off his front. He wouldn't say the sensation was pleasant, but keeping the hair growth under control was the key.

"Ouch," Tony said, observing the task. He yanked his shirt over his head revealing the smooth bronze skin of his chest. "Glad Clare helped me shave this morning. That looks like some serious hurt."

Royce clamped his jaw tight then jerked the corner of the last pad on his pec. Tossing the used strip in the wastebasket sitting atop the desk, he reached for his shirt. "You missed the fun part." He tapped a spot high on his left thigh about as close to his junk as it could be without him removing his underwear. "This is the worst one. Hair or no hair. Hurts like a son of a bitch every time."

Tony's hand went to the same spot on his own leg. Pulling his shorts on, Royce chuckled.

Tricia dug in her big bag, came out with a new box of electrode pads. "Don't let him scare you, Tony. When it comes to pain, Royce can dish it out, but he can't take it."

He couldn't believe her comment. He was sure she didn't mean it to sound the way it did, but he couldn't say the same for Tony.

Ramirez cut his eyes to Royce. One side of his mouth raised in a smirk. "Is that so? Like to make 'em scream, Strikeout?"

"I've made my share of batters scream in frustration."

"Not lately." Tony hooked his thumbs in his shorts waistband, shoving them down to his ankles.

Royce had to do something with his hands to keep from punching the smartass in the mouth. He grabbed his shoes off the floor and, without sparing his teammate another look, he stormed out of the office.

CHAPTER ELEVEN

"What was that all about?"

"Nothing. I was just pushing his buttons. He'll get over it."

"I certainly hope so." She needed Royce in her study. Of all the potential players the Mustangs had offered her, his problem seemed the one most likely to benefit from her research. If she could find something...*anything* to help the man get back on his game, everything she'd sacrificed for her research would be worth it. And not just because positive results would be a great marketing tool, but because she wanted to see Royce succeed.

Her feelings for the man were as far from rational and objective as they could be, and she'd known him for less than a week! It made no sense, but that's the way it was.

"If it's okay with you, I'm going to get the baseline readings first, then we should have time to rig you up with the wireless sensors, too. You wear those during the game so I get real, game-time readings to compare with the baseline ones."

"My body is yours to do with as you please. Clare said to

tell you, if the jock strap covers it to keep your hands off, otherwise, have fun."

Tricia laughed out loud. "I can't wait to meet your wife. She sounds like one of a kind."

"You don't know how true those words are. Clare Kincaid Ramirez is a rare diamond."

Tricia's fingers stilled on the box of pads she'd picked up. The reverence in Tony's voice when he spoke of his wife nearly brought tears to her eyes. She hoped Clare knew how lucky she was. Royce instantly came to mind. The things he'd done to her body had set the bar high for future lovers. It was too bad the man didn't appreciate the other things she had going for her, because she was afraid she was one kiss away from thinking of him the way Tony thought of Clare. And that just wouldn't do.

No more kisses. No more orgasms—at least none courtesy of Royce Stryker. She wouldn't think of the man behind the baseball player. The one who'd bought a home instead of a house then refused to let someone who didn't know him decorate it. Or the man who'd asked nothing for himself, but gave her what she needed when she hadn't known she needed anything—much less *that*.

He was hurting inside. It didn't take a psychologist to see his divorce had rocked his confidence and led to a breakdown in his professional life as well. If she could get enough data, she was sure she could isolate the muscle groups he needed to concentrate on in order to get back on track. Once he got his professional life in order, no doubt he'd be back in the saddle, so to speak, too. He'd ride off into the sunset with the hot babe of the day, leaving her and her computer program in the dirt.

Mentally slapping the dust cloud out of her brain, she unwrapped the first of many electrode pads and turned to Mustangs' Test Subject #2. "You shouldn't tease him about his pitching. It won't help him get back in form."

"Maybe not."

Tricia adhered the first pad just above Tony's left nipple then reached into the box for more of the individually wrapped packages. She kept one for herself and handed the rest to Tony. "Here. Open these. That will speed things up."

They worked in tandem for a few minutes, Tony unwrapping then handing the sticky pads to Tricia to slap on his skin.

"You always this gentle?"

Kneeling in front of him, she looked up.

His eyebrows were knit in confusion. "If you want to slap somebody around, I'll call Strikeout back in here. He's riding the bench today. Me? I've got to play, and it's hard enough without being used as a punching bag before the game."

She ducked her head and, placing her hands on the floor, pushed to her feet. "I'm sorry, Tony. It's just…."

"Strikeout? You and Royce got something goin' on? If the scumbag is leaving you unsatisfied, I'll set him straight."

"Oh God." She grabbed Tony's arm and squeezed. The last thing she needed was this man going to bat for her with Royce. "No. Please don't say anything to him. It's nothing like what you're thinking."

"I knew something was going on between you two. The man has it bad for you."

Tricia froze as her new guinea pig's words registered. Hope flared hot and bright in her chest like a sparkler on the Fourth of July, but fizzled out just as fast.

"Please don't say anything to him. I'll be out of his life in a few weeks, and he'll forget all about me."

Tony cleared a spot and sat on the corner of the desk. "You're really hung up on him, aren't you?"

She nodded. "Yeah. But I don't think he feels the same, and I have no right to expect him to. Besides, I have a job to do here, and a personal relationship with one of my test subjects could jeopardize my project."

"First, it's plain to anyone with eyes Strikeout is nuts about you. So much so, it's making him crazy. Yesterday, he basically told me to stay away from you, and that scene a few minutes ago? All because I didn't listen to him and stay away."

Tricia applied a pad to his right calf, this time smoothing the edges down with a touch so light, he could understand Royce's interest. If Tony didn't have Clare waiting at home to make his skin quiver, he'd sure as hell respond to Tricia's touch. "Thanks for ignoring him," she said, reaching her hand up. Tony placed the pad he'd just unwrapped in her palm and set about opening another one. "I hope he doesn't succeed in scaring off others. I need several more players to participate, or the findings won't mean anything."

"You tell me who's next in line, and I'll make sure they show up." She didn't respond to his offer, just continued silently placing pad after pad until he looked like a pair of jeans, patched too many times to wear.

"You think you can find something to help Royce get back on his game?" he asked while she attached wires to the electrodes dotting his body.

"I hope I can. I'd hate to think a man's career could be ended simply because he isn't using a specific muscle group to its best advantage." She hooked a wire to an electrode on his left shoulder blade.

"What about me? I'm playing just fine. Shouldn't you be testing players who aren't doing so well?"

"There's always room for improvement." She clamped another wire to a pad on his biceps. "You may think you're playing to the best of your ability, but my research thus far suggests athletes know very little about their own bodies and how they move."

Tony nodded. "Yeah, I can see your point. So, you're saying this computer program of yours can help anyone, not just a player going through a periodic slump."

"That's what I'm saying. If the program works, it could eradicate the occasional slump from the game entirely, as well as indicate when a player is in an irreversible decline as opposed to a slump."

If her program even came close to working, it would change professional sports across the board. From a player's standpoint, it could prolong his career, or end it prematurely, depending on what team owners did with the information acquired from the players. Fuck.

He asked a few more questions while she continued to hook him up to her computer. Concentrating on her work, she didn't seem to be holding anything back in her answers. He genuinely believed her when she talked about using her research to benefit wounded soldiers and civilians facing physical challenges. All that was fine and good, but so was nuclear power unless it ended up in the hands of someone with no moral compass.

MLB and the team owners were without morals, but they controlled the money, and with it, the players' lives. Technological advances over the years had changed the face of the game in many ways—stadium lighting, enclosed stadiums, better bases, equipment, and safety gear. Hell, television coverage and, now, the instant replay had altered the game. But mostly, the players had remained untouched. There was Tommy John surgery, a miracle medical procedure that had saved many pitching careers in the last two decades, but, not much else had touched the human factor of the game. If Dr. Reed's computer program did what she hoped it would do, he could see owners using the tool as a means to select players, ensuring they had only the best of the best on their roster.

Of course, that's what they tried to do now, but the decisions were based on many factors, not scientific analysis of the person's physical abilities and limitations. What about personality or eagerness or flat-out hunger for a World Championship? Those were the kinds of things a computer program couldn't measure, yet they could be the difference between a good player and an exceptional player.

Tony followed Tricia's instructions, allowing her to collect the data she needed regarding his off-the-field fitness level. Ripping off the first set of electrodes was every bit as unpleasant as Royce indicated it would be then he stood before the good doctor once again in nothing but his jock strap while she applied a set of wireless transmitters he would wear while playing.

Fuck. He needed to talk to Strikeout, see if the man shared his concerns about Tricia's research. Maybe Tony was paranoid, but he didn't think so.

"Would you call this medical research?" he asked, carefully tugging his practice uniform on so as not to dislodge any of the porcupine-esque wires attached to his skin.

"Most definitely." Tricia tapped the keys on her laptop, her gaze glued to the small, rectangular screen.

"Who do you see using this, in the League, I mean? Team doctors, physical therapists, trainers?"

"All of the above and the players themselves."

"What about management?"

She looked up at him. "What about management? I don't see the information being of any use to them other than to help their players perform to the best of their ability."

Which answered his question. It hadn't occurred to Dr. Reed that her project could be used to manipulate careers or in the grand scheme, to change the game by putting a crop of emotionless, physically-fit robots on the field in place of human beings.

He could tell by the look on Ramirez's face as he strode across the dugout toward him that Tricia had convinced the man to wear the wireless sensors for today's game. Royce knew firsthand how those things could pinch as your body moved in the normal range of motion.

Tony rubbed the top of his thigh and instantly Strike remembered the day that particular electrode had malfunctioned on him. *Christ.* The idea of Tricia doing to Tony what she'd done to him made him see red before he forced rational thoughts to take over. Ramirez was married, very happily so it seemed. The idea of her seeing and touching Tony…shit. The thought fucked with his sanity.

"Come with me." Ramirez barked the order as he passed Royce in the nearly empty pre-game dugout and headed into the tunnel leading to the clubhouse.

What the fuck? Out of curiosity, he followed. When Tony

opened the door to the very same supply closet where things had gone beyond heated to explosive with Tricia, and motioned him inside, Royce balked. "You got problems with the equipment, you fix it yourself." He turned to head back out to watch batting practice only to have Tony's hand clamp down on his elbow, stopping him.

"Get in here. Now. We need to talk." Surprised at the usually jovial man's angry tone, Royce glanced up and down the hallway to make sure no one was around then stepped into the closet.

"What the fuck, man?"

"Have you given any thought to this research bullshit?" Tony stood with his hands fisted on his hips. Royce had never seen his teammate this pissed off.

"Tricia's research?"

"What the fuck else would I be talking about? Do you have any idea what this could mean if she succeeds and it ends up in the owner's hands? We'll all be out of a fuckin' job. There won't be anyone on the field except perfect fuckin' robots. We've got to put a stop to this. Now. Before she comes up with something concrete."

"Whoa." Royce held up a hand to stop Tony's rant. "Stop right there. *We* aren't going to do anything to stop Tricia's research." He waved his index finger between them. "*You and I* are going to wear her fuckin' electrodes so she can collect whatever fuckin' readings she wants. Then you're going to stay the fuck away from her."

"Seriously? Are you even listening to yourself? You're so much in love with the woman, you can't see what's going on here." Tony jabbed a finger in the center of Royce's chest. "Fuckin' management is using her research to screw us all out of our contracts."

Royce was so hung up on Tony's assertion he was in love with Tricia, he almost missed the last part of the man's statement. "What the fuck are you talking about? You think management is using her?"

Ramirez explained his thoughts, ending with his belief that

Dr. Reed was completely innocent in regards to his conspiracy theory.

Royce gripped the corner of the metal shelving to keep himself upright. "I should have seen it. I don't know why I didn't."

"Like I said, you're in love with the woman. *She's* all you can see right now." Tony clapped Royce on the back. "I don't blame you a bit. If I didn't have Clare, I'd probably make a run at Tricia myself."

Royce glared at the other man. "I am not in love or anything else with Dr. Reed."

Tony backed to the other side of the small room. "Deny it all you want, man, but I call 'em like I see 'em. Besides, I'm totally monogamous now. Clare is more than enough for one man."

"Fuck, man. I *do not* want to hear about your kinky love life. Keep that shit to yourself, okay?"

Ramirez laughed. "I didn't say…. Hell, forget I said anything at all. We need to figure out what we're going to do about this. If Dr. Reed's program can do what she thinks it can, then we can't let management get their hands on it. Talk about bad—all the way around."

Doyle hadn't specifically told him not to discuss his dual role as both guinea pig and spy, but since the program wasn't common knowledge among the players, he could only assume he needed to keep the manager's confidence. That meant playing dumb for Tony. "Can't you go to Doyle? Isn't he a relative or something now?"

"He's Clare's uncle." Tony scraped a hand over his face. "Shit. I can't believe he'd be involved in something like this. He's always struck me as one of the good guys, you know? On the player's side.

Royce nodded. "I agree. Maybe you should talk to him, see what he has to say." With a little luck, his uncle would fill him in. He didn't feel right about keeping things from Tony, especially when he could see how upset the guy was over the situation.

"Shit. He loves the game as much as anybody I've ever known." He shook his head. "I just can't see him agreeing to something like this."

Again, Royce nodded. Unable to agree or disagree, Royce stared at the floor. "You have any ideas?"

"Not a one. You?"

Tricia had poured everything into her work, the idea of doing anything to stop her made him sick to his stomach, but Tony was right, if there was a chance her program could negatively impact the players in baseball or any sport, then he'd have no choice but to turn the information over to Doyle and let him go up against the League to squash her project. "Let me think about it. We're the only two players involved right now, and hell, we don't have a clue if her program will even work. If it doesn't, then there's no problem, right?"

"Right."

"Then why don't we go on about our business, let Tricia do her research. I don't even want to think about sabotaging her work, or whatever the hell else we could do to stop her, until she actually has something the League could want."

"I agree. In the meantime, let's try to figure a way out of this that doesn't ruin baseball and, hell, every other professional sport out there, just in case." Ramirez grabbed the doorknob, but before he opened the door, he turned back to Royce. "Stay close to her, Strike. If she comes up with anything, you'll be the first person she tells."

He felt as if he had a candy fireball lodged in his throat. "Sure. I'll stay close to her. Not a problem." Never mind he'd just told her he wouldn't touch her until their month was up. That had to be the stupidest thing he'd ever done in his life. Tony was wrong about one thing—he wasn't in love with Tricia. He knew what love was. The thing between him and Tricia was physical, nothing more.

Royce grabbed the edge of a shoulder-high shelf. His head was a dead weight hanging between his shoulders, dragging him down into a cesspool of lies that could only lead to disaster.

"Fuck! Fuck! Fuck!" He took his frustration out on the rack, causing the bottles of cleaning supplies to totter. A broom handle dislodged from its resting place and clattered to the floor. His relationship with her was built on lies and deceit. It didn't take a genius to figure out how Tricia would react if she found out what he was up to, and the only way she wouldn't find out was if her research flopped.

Best case scenario—her project fails. Then she'll never know you weren't going to let it succeed anyway.

That's fucked up, even for you.

Royce peeled his fingers off the shelf, rolled his shoulders to release the tension holding him in like a vise. He inhaled, counting to ten before letting the stale air whoosh from his lungs. Spending time with Dr. Reed wouldn't be a problem. She seemed as eager as he to see where their physical attraction would take them. He admired her intellect, finding her brain as sexy as her body. The way she trusted him made him feel like a god—a lying, no-good bastard of a god, but a god nonetheless.

After repeating the shoulder roll and deep breathing exercises a few more times, he regained enough control to go out in public again. There was the usual pre-game chaos in the dugout. Players going through rituals that could be signs of OCD but were definitely superstition. Royce skirted past Tony, who stood in front of the cubbyholes containing their batting helmets, cursing a blue streak because someone had turned his helmet to face the wrong way. Baseball players were a strange lot, believing things as inconsequential as the way their equipment was stowed to where they sat on the bench could make a difference in their performance on the field.

Royce took a seat at the far end of the bench where he could watch the introductions and such at home plate as well as observe his teammates' game preparations. They were a quirky bunch, no doubt about it, but each one of them brought something unique to the team. It wasn't just their strong points on the field, but their weaknesses, too, that made them assets to the team. Take Jeff Holder, for example. No one gave a shit if he couldn't throw a curve ball to save his hide. His hundred-mile-per-hour fastball had made him the best closer in the league. In a perfect-player world, there wasn't room for a one-pitch pitcher. But take Holder out of the last inning, and you'd take away the excitement of the game—those nail-biting three outs, where the opposing team knew they were facing their greatest competition yet, and thus, played their hardest. It's what fans and players alike lived for, the rush of anticipation, the feeling that anything could happen.

Anything can happen.

Images of Tricia on her knees, her rose-colored lips wrapped around his cock, came to mind. *Anything can happen.* Like a pixy, all brains and innocence could show up and take him for the ride of his life. Now, he just had to figure out how to keep his pixy from finding out she'd placed her trust in the wrong man.

CHAPTER TWELVE

The data stream from the sensors attached to Tony Ramirez was better than Tricia had hoped for. It would take days, if not weeks, to compare the game readings to the ones she'd taken under controlled conditions. With two subjects to work at her disposal, she couldn't wait to get into the analysis part of the research. She'd done some preliminary work on the data collected from Royce. There was something there, but what that something was she hadn't a clue.

Royce's problems were obvious. His pitches weren't going where they were supposed to. The question was, why? What was he doing different than when his pitches were perfectly under his control? Without a data set from before he lost the strike zone, she'd have to compare the pitches still going where they were supposed to against the rogue ones.

With Tony, she had a different set of problems. His game seemed to be perfect now, so what, if anything, could he do to improve on his already flawless performance?

Tricia tapped her stylus against the iPad she'd been using to make notes to herself while she watched the game and the incoming data stream simultaneously. Both situations were exactly the kind she'd hoped her program would address, but first, she had to find something in the massive amounts of data she was collecting that would make a difference in the players' performances. She'd had a few successes with the college players she'd worked with early on, but they'd been so young and just about any constructive criticism regarding their playing could make a difference. These were professionals she was working with now. Men who had reached the pinnacle of their careers, whose bodies were well-maintained machines, finely tuned to run at optimum performance levels. Finding a flaw of any kind would be damn near impossible. Getting them to concentrate on a specific muscle or group of muscles in order to change something might be the hardest task of all. These men didn't *think* they just *moved*.

Talk about moves. She smiled to herself, remembering the way Royce had moved when his cock had been in her mouth. There was absolutely nothing wrong with the man's hips. He could rock them with controlled precision without giving it a thought.

Tricia closed her eyes, imagining the way he would make love—all that contained power gliding gracefully over and inside her body. He'd know what he was doing, unlike the fumbling guys she'd been with in the past. Boys pretending to be men. Boys who didn't know any more about their own bodies than they did about hers.

She'd give Royce an A+ in female anatomy. He knew where all her buttons were, and how to push them. All the more reason to keep her distance from him. She had no choice but to take full responsibility for initiating the intimacies between them. She wasn't proud of what she'd done, but she would live with it. She'd put both their careers in jeopardy because of one stupid, hormone-driven, impulsive action.

Going home instead of meeting him after yesterday's game had been the right thing to do. Thank God, Royce had come around to her way of thinking, too. If he launched even a half-hearted attempt to persuade her into his bed, her resolve would crumble. Give her another one of those orgasms he did so well and he'd be dusting what was left of her off his sheets like so many cracker crumbs.

"Pathetic," she mumbled. The game had been over for more than an hour. The stadium would be emptying out, the staff and players heading home for a good night's sleep before embarking on a ten-day road trip in the morning.

Closing her laptop, she stood and began stuffing reports into her briefcase. She'd have plenty to do on the plane, but first she needed to get home and pack.

"Going somewhere?"

The deep, masculine voice startled her. Hand over her pounding heart, she looked at the man standing in the doorway. Why did he have to look so damn good? One glimpse of his long legs and wide shoulders lounging in her doorway and she could feel her determination flaking away. "Royce! You scared me."

"Didn't mean to."

"Well, you did." As she continued to pack up her materials, he remained where he was, stalking her with his eyes. The heat level in the room had gone up so much a bead of sweat trickled down her spine. "Do you need something?"

A harsh bark of laughter made her jerk her head up. "What?"

"Funny you should put it that way. Do I need something?" His eyes narrowed. With laser precision, he zeroed in on her crotch. "I need you."

Need, hot, heavy, suffocating in its intensity, seized her body. She couldn't breathe for the weight pressing down on her chest. Her knees gave out, and she sank into her desk chair. Every reason she shouldn't give in to her overpowering attraction to this man flashed through her brain, each one incinerated by a blast of lust before she could grasp onto the lifeline it represented. Before she crumbled completely, she managed one scrap of sane thought. "What happened to waiting until the end of the month?"

"I changed my mind." He approached the desk like a wolf

circling wounded prey. "Neither one of us was going to make it three more weeks. I won't make it three more hours." He finished stuffing her laptop into her bag, hefted the strap to his shoulder, and reached his hand out to her. "Let's go."

Tricia stared at his palm. If she put her hand in his, there would be no turning back. No pretending they could maintain a strictly professional relationship. Her research where he was concerned would be compromised beyond inclusion in the study.

"No more thinking. Only feeling, Patricia." He wiggled his fingers. "Come."

Come. The single syllable reverberated through her charged system like an atom in an atomic accelerator. Her core went into nuclear meltdown. She squeezed her thighs together in an effort to keep her body from following his order as given.

She lifted her hand, touched her fingers to his. The strength of his hand encompassing hers was both comfort and torture. He tugged her to her feet. The smile curving his lips and twinkle in his eyes suggested he knew the battle she was fighting. "Not here, babe. Not like this."

The drive to his house was accomplished in silence. He continued to hold her hand, pressing her palm against his wool-clad thigh. She wasn't sure if he meant to keep her from touching herself or if his intent was to remind her of her decision. Like she could forget.

Her body hummed right along with the powerful car propelling them through the night. The only difference was, the car observed the speed limit while her system ran full throttle, seemingly without brakes.

They turned onto his driveway. "Open the gate."

She followed his gaze to the remote opener clipped to the sun visor on her side. Using her free hand, she pushed the button. The ornate iron gates swung slowly open. Once through, she glanced over her shoulder. The massive gates sealed them inside Royce Stryker's private world.

No turning back. He squeezed her fingers, commanding her attention away from the past. She'd chosen this path, however ill-advised it might be. With a clarity she hadn't possessed since the day she met Royce, she realized it wasn't the iron barrier behind her blocking her escape—it was her need to be with this man, to give herself to him completely. It might have been his voice, his will, compelling her to go with him this evening, but it was *her* will and *her* inner voice keeping her from demanding he take her home.

She sat, her hands loose in her lap until he came around the front of the car to open her door. When he reached for her, she let him help her from the car. They entered his house via the same door they'd used the one other time she'd been there, but instead of stopping in the rooms she was familiar with, he ushered her up a wide, curved staircase at the front of the house.

The master suite was enormous, taking up close to half of the second floor. Her sense of direction told her the tall casement windows looked out on the backyard and the far end of the house she had yet to see. In the few seconds before he pushed her up against the back of the bedroom door, blocking her view of anything but him, she'd noted the large four-poster bed, off center in the room. The color scheme, mostly dark reds with black and some gold splashes was masculine but tasteful.

"I've wanted you in this room since the day we met." Still holding her hand in his, he lifted it above her head while his other hand went to her waist. She closed her eyes, melting into him when his lips found the sensitive spot behind her ear and began to devour her.

He took his time, licking, nibbling, kissing her neck, her jaw, and finally, her mouth. His tongue demanded entrance, and with a sigh, she allowed it. But instead of letting him take while she gave, she dueled back, insisting on learning the taste of him as well. They were both breathless by the time they finally broke apart. When she dared to open her eyes, she found him studying her face, his eyebrows knitted in concentration as if he didn't know what to make of her.

"Did I do something wrong?" Because of the way she'd

sucked his cock the other day, he probably assumed she had more experience than she did. But how could she have kissed wrong?

"No." His voice had a hard edge to it, sending shivers of anticipation down her spine. "I'm just trying to figure out what I'm going to do to you first."

"What do you mean?" She licked her lips. "W-what are your choices?"

He traced her lips with his thumb, pausing to tug her lower lip down then pinch it lightly. It was a silly gesture, but it made other parts of her beg for the same treatment.

"There are so many choices, sweetheart, and my brain is working on some I'm sure haven't even been invented yet." His fingers skimmed her jaw then down her neck to the ribbed neck of her shirt. "First things first, though." Grabbing her shoulders, he spun her around. "Drop your shorts and brace yourself on the bed. I owe you a spanking for not showing up the other night."

"You deserved that." She glanced over her shoulder at him, but he wouldn't be swayed by logic.

"Yes, and you deserve this, too." He didn't know where he'd found the edgy voice he was using, but from the way her eyes dilated, it was having the desired effect. She was as turned on as he was. "Drop them. This won't take long then we'll explore all my other choices for the night."

His dick was going to poke a hole through his trousers if he wasn't careful. Even worse, he was close to coming in his pants just from watching her obediently wiggle out of her shorts and bend over the bed. She had the cutest ass he'd ever seen. Those soft, round globes were made to be spanked.

He put one hand in the center of her back and raised the other over his head.

"I expected you to meet me after the game." *Whack!* She cried out and dug her fingers into his bedspread.

"I looked for you." *Whack!* "You weren't in your office." *Whack!* Her head thrashed from side to side.

"I stood outside your apartment." *Whack!* She jerked her

head up. Clearly, this was news to her. "Debating whether I should spank you right then." *Whack!* She buried her face in the comforter.

"I fuckin' had to jerk off in the shower." *Whack!* "Alone." *Whack!* A strangled sob broke from her lips.

"The next day, I found out you were playing games with me." *Whack!* "Fair is fair." *Whack!*

"Your ass is mine." *Whack!*

His mental tally reached ten, and he stopped to admire his handiwork. Beneath the hand pressing her into the mattress, he could feel her breath coming in shallow pants of arousal. Her skin glowed red, and the scent wafting from between her legs was heavy with desire. He could take her fast and hard, right where she was, but he had better plans for the evening. Now that they'd gotten the discipline out of the way, they had nothing but time.

He stepped closer, pressing his erection into her hip and cupping her butt with his hand. Good God, the heat coming off her skin roused the caveman inside him. He called on the same control he used during a game to keep himself in check. "You won't leave me aching again, will you, sweetheart?"

"No, sir."

"I'll always be fair, Tricia. I'll always give you what you need." He stroked her reddened flesh in an effort to take the sting out of her punishment, giving himself time to step back from the edge. He had every intention of ravishing her, but he was going to take his time doing it so she'd understand what she'd denied them both the other night.

He couldn't help himself. He moved behind her, gripped her hips, and ground the thick ridge of his erection into her cleft. Her fingers clutched at the bedclothes each time he moved against her. At last, he stepped back. "Pull your pants up and turn around."

When she turned around, her face was almost as red as her ass. She'd shed a few tears, but mostly, she looked more aroused than anything.

"Did I hurt you?" He reached up to feel the heat on her

cheek. It reminded him so much of the blush he'd put on her butt.

"Yes." For an instant, he hated his need to spank her, but then her lips curved up on the corners, and he knew she was toying with him. "But I liked it."

"Good God, woman." He took her in his arms, one hand moving low to cup her bottom. He pressed his cheek against her temple. "You'll pay for scaring me that way."

"I hope so."

He groaned. She would be the death of him, no doubt about it. "Don't think I'll forget about your impertinence, young lady. But tonight, there are other things I want to do to you."

"What kind of things?"

As much as he hated to let go of her, he needed to see her reaction to his words. He released his hold on her, putting a few inches of space between them. "I think I'll start by licking my way down one side of your body then back up the other. Sort of a road trip, with a few in-depth sightseeing tours along the way."

He drew the back of his hand across her breasts. Her nipples, already peeking out, hardened to diamond points. The change didn't escape his attention. He stroked his thumb over one then the other. His gaze, however, remained locked on hers. "I want to suck these. Tell me, what color are they?"

"I…don't know." Her mind was still reeling from the spanking and then the tender way he'd held her afterwards, as if she were something precious. She'd always been way ahead of other kids, intellectually, and because of her uniqueness, she'd been treated differently than most children. Her parents didn't know what to do with her, so they'd done nothing at all. They loved her, she was sure of that, but the few times she'd acted out, instead of scolding her or giving her a spanking, they'd shrugged and chalked her behavior up to her curious mind. Deep down, she'd known her mini rebellions had been pleas for attention.

She'd had Royce Stryker's attention from the beginning, and he had no qualms at all about calling her on her misbehavior. She was almost giddy, thinking her teasing comments had earned her another spanking.

"You know what color they are. You see them every day." He pinched her left one between his thumb and forefinger, bringing his question into sharp focus. "Tell me."

Tricia closed her eyes, bringing an image of her own body to mind. "Pink. Rose, maybe."

He turned his attention to the other one, giving it a pinch, too. "Your pussy is the same, sweet color." He brushed his lips over hers. "I can't wait to see it up close again. I want to make you come all over my tongue."

She could barely breathe. What he described scared her out of her mind. "I want that, too," she confessed on a whisper. Daring to open her eyes, she looked up. Everything she felt was mirrored in Royce's eyes—lust, longing, need, desperation. He dipped his head. Her gaze dropped to his parted lips descending toward hers.

He'd never wanted a woman the way he wanted this one. He'd only ever been with Hannah, but the kind of sex he'd had with his ex-wife seemed tame compared to the things he wanted to do with Tricia. He'd never once wanted to spank Hannah, but every time he got near Tricia, his hand itched to redden her bottom.

The woman had bewitched him. There was no other explanation for the way his body reacted to her. He needed her. Craved her. Staying away from her wasn't an option, even though he'd tried to convince himself it was. That she would give herself to him in such an open and honest way, humbled him.

In the back of his mind, he knew ultimately he might destroy her by sabotaging her work, but right now, all he could think about was possessing her, mind, body, and soul. As his lips covered hers, seducing and being seduced, one word echoed in his brain, drowning out reason, sanity, and especially his conscience. *Mine.*

Curving his palms beneath her ass, he half-carried, half walked her to the bed. Finesse took a backseat to need as their clothes came off in record time. He helped her scoot out of her shorts and panties then sat back on his heels to admire her.

"God, you are the most beautiful woman I have ever seen." Rose nipples. His mouth watered to taste them. His gaze traveled every womanly inch of her, pausing at the soft mound at the nexus of her thighs. His fingers twitched, remembering the wet warmth waiting there for him. He wanted so badly to fall on her, to part her legs and drive himself inside her, to claim her, but he forced himself to proceed at a slower pace. Gently clasping her ankles, he spread her just enough so he could wedge his knees between hers. Using his forearms for support so he wouldn't squash her, he fit his body over hers. He groaned as his cock became trapped between their bodies, his hard and unforgiving, hers so damn soft and welcoming he wanted to cry.

She wrapped her arms around his shoulders and tugged. Letting his arms slide forward, he lowered his chest to hers, groaning at the feel of her breasts absorbing his weight. Her nipples were hard little nubs, poking holes in his restraint. "You feel so damn good I could stay here all night."

He stroked the top of her head with both hands as his gaze searched her face. Her eyes were luminous pools, inviting him in. Her lips, swollen from his kisses, parted on a sigh. "Royce?"

"What baby? What do you need?"

"You said you were going to lick me all over."

He failed to contain a burst of laughter. Leave it to the brainiac to remind him of his promises. "I did promise you, didn't I?"

"Yes, you did. And I've been waiting a long time, don't you think?"

"Too long," he agreed. "Way too long."

The swipe of his tongue from the base of her neck to her earlobe made her entire body shimmy with need. She moved her hands from his shoulders to his head, holding on tight as he moved over her chest. As he inched his way toward her breasts, she braced herself for the moment he would put his mouth on them. Nothing could have prepared her for the reality of it. At first, he teased her nipples, flicking his tongue over one then the other until they were so hard they ached.

"Please." If he didn't ease the ache, she was going to die.

"Patience."

She squirmed beneath him and tugged on his head, but he refused to pick up the pace. He continued to torture her breasts, nipping at the tight tips then kissing away the flair of pain with soft lips and a soothing tongue. When he finally sucked one into his mouth, she dug her fingernails into his scalp and arched her neck and back.

"Royce!" *Oh. My. God.* Every pull on her breast telegraphed lightning to her womb. Her pussy clenched, and her hips seemed to have acquired a mind of their own. She ground against him, could not get close enough to him to satisfy the clawing need inside her body.

When he released her breast, she sagged with relief, only to be thrown back into the pit of desire when he turned his attention to the other one.

She wanted. She needed. Something nameless and powerful held her in its grip. Whatever it was, she knew without a doubt Royce Stryker was the cause of it, just like he was the only man in the world who could make it go away.

God, he loved the way she moved underneath him, as if she wanted to crawl inside him. He couldn't get enough of her, either. The first taste of her skin, and he'd become an addict. He had every intention of doing as he promised, licking every inch of her, but as soon as he took her breast into his mouth, felt her nipple flatten on the roof of his mouth, he knew he was doomed to failure, at least for today. He'd get around to the rest of her delectable body eventually, but for the moment, he had to taste the essence of her. Had to drink her in, had to feel her come in his mouth. Maybe after he did, he could find the patience he'd asked of her, and fulfill his promise.

He felt sure he was going to have claw marks on his scalp, but decided it was a small price to pay for what he was going to receive in return. Tricia held on as he made his way down her torso, stopping to tease her belly button with his tongue before pausing over her mound to inhale the musk of her arousal. Shifting farther down on the bed, he urged her legs wider. She hesitated for a heartbeat then spread her thighs wider.

If he hadn't already been lying down, the sight of her pussy flowering open for him would have felled him. *Holy Hell.* He'd found the pearly gates. Moist, pink lips guarded Heaven and begged for his kiss. His cock jerked, demanding immediate access. Ignoring the discomfort in his groin, he pressed his nose into the uppermost juncture of her outer lips and drew in her scent.

He'd turned into a caveman. His body wanted. Need hammered between his legs. His balls felt ready to explode.

Mine. Mine. Mine.

The mantra repeated in every cell of his body.

As he drew his tongue over her pussy, he silently vowed to do everything he could to protect what was his.

Tricia gasped. Her hips came off the mattress, undulating in an attempt to either get away or get closer, she wasn't entirely sure which. With her fingers still clinging to his scalp, she crunched her abs, lifting herself. A wave of acute embarrassment washed over her. Would she ever get used to seeing his head buried between her legs? He flicked his tongue over her clitoris and thinking wasn't an option any longer.

Her head fell back against the bed, and she forgot all about coming up with reasons Royce Stryker should not have his face between her legs.

He was a master with his tongue, using it in ways she wouldn't have dreamed possible to bring her to the brink then coax her back down again, only to start the whole process over.

She was going insane, one lick, one suck, one forbidden

penetration at a time. She tugged on his hair until, without stopping his assault on her senses, he pried her fingers loose and guided her hands down to the bed on either side of her hips. Digging her fingers into the covers, she held on with a white-knuckled grip to keep from flying off the roller coaster.

Nothing so *bad* had ever felt so good. Even the sounds made her crazy. There was the occasional *pop* when he broke suction on her clit. Then there were the wet, slurping noises—positively obscene. The worst ones seemed to originate deep in his chest and came out as grunts and moans that vibrated through her and sent tingles along every nerve ending in her body and wound her insides tight.

"Please." He held her on the precipice…so close. So damn close. "Please, Royce."

She felt his smile, thought she heard him laugh. Then he plunged two fingers inside her tight channel, and with the skill of a man who knew what he was looking for, crooked the tips upward. Two taps against her secret button, and she left the launch pad.

As her hips rocketed skyward, Tricia dug her heels into the mattress. The muscles in her stomach and abdomen jerked, clenching and releasing in breath stealing.

Oh God. Oh God. Oh God.

"You okay, babe?"

Tricia opened her eyes to see Royce braced above her, a knowing smirk on his face. Tremors still racked her body from her ribcage to the tingling flesh between her legs. She didn't trust her voice to not utter ridiculous words of love, so she nodded.

"I'm clean, but I didn't know about birth control, so I grabbed a condom."

Her mind whirled. When? How?

He flexed his hips, bringing the head of his cock to her entrance. "I need you," he said, nudging inside a fraction, just enough to let her feel the stretch required to take all of him. "Say something, sweetheart. Yes or no."

Yes! Yes! Yes! She brought her knees up to bracket his hips.

He fit in the notch of her legs like a puzzle piece. She let go of the sheet and wrapped her hands over his shoulders, loving the feel of strong muscles bunched tight to keep him suspended above her. But she wanted more. She wanted all of him—his weight pressing her into the mattress, his cock filling all the empty spaces inside her. She'd never wanted anything more.

She looped her legs around his thighs, anchoring him where she wanted him. She looked up into his face lined with strain and uncertainty, and her heart hammered against her rib cage. She opened herself to him, body and soul. When her gaze locked with his, she gave him the permission he sought. "Yes."

He entered her with one slow thrust, tunneling into her sweet, wet heat as carefully as possible given the voice in his head urging him to hammer into her until he went blind with his release. Lord, she was the tightest, wettest, most perfect fit ever. It took every ounce of self-control he had to deny his need. Her gaze remained locked on his, her eyes widening at first then slowly her lids dropped. A soft sigh escaped her parted lips. Her hips rose off the bed, taking more of him inside. She tipped her head back, exposing the long column of her neck in surrender.

He bent and kissed his way from her collarbone to her jaw, silently claiming what was his while holding perfectly still inside her. She needed time to adjust to his size, and he needed time to wrap his head around his new reality. He had to have her, and not just for a short fling. She was his, and he'd move heaven and earth to keep her.

"Royce."

"You feel so good." He covered her mouth with his, groaning when their tongues dueled. Her sexy little moan incinerated his control. Withdrawing, he slammed back into her. She made another noise that sounded like approval to his ringing ears. He pulled his lips from hers, and somehow found enough restraint to wait until she lifted her gaze to his.

"I need you. Now. You ready?"

"Please, Royce." Her legs tightened around his, anchoring

him in place. "Don't make me wait another second."

He knew his smile was feral, but the need in her voice mirrored the desperation he felt inside. Pulling back so only the tip of his cock opened her, he held her gaze for the length of a heartbeat before he gave them both what they wanted.

She took all of him, rising to meet his thrusts, keeping the pace he'd set. As much as she needed to feel him filling her over and over again, every time he sank deep inside her, she dug her nails into his ass in a futile effort to keep him there. Nothing had ever felt as good or as right as when their bodies fused completely.

Emotions she had no business having filled her heart to overflowing. She closed her eyes and focused everything she had on the point where they were no longer individuals but one single entity with two hearts beating in tandem. She was probably nothing more than a sexual partner to him, but he was so much more to her. He'd tire of her soon enough, but she knew at her core there would never be another person who made her feel the way Royce did.

His cock stroked her pussy in long, powerful movements. On an elemental level, she was his—always would be. Everywhere he touched her, her skin hummed as if awakened from a deep sleep. She wanted things with him she'd never dreamed of with anyone else. She wanted to be naughty, so he would spank her. She wanted to drop to her knees and wrap her lips around his shaft. She wanted to come for him the way she had before, kneeling at his feet or lying across his lap or beneath him, taking him inside her, giving her body to him. She wanted it all.

"You feel so damn good." Supporting himself on one arm, he cupped her breast in his big, rough hand then bent to take her puckered nipple into his mouth. His tongue teased the aching bud, and she arched her back, silently begging for more. He obliged, sucking hard. She knew enough about the female anatomy to know there was no direct connection between her breasts and her pussy, but it was as if his mouth clamped to her tit completed some secret circuit of nerve endings. Pleasure arced from point of contact to point of contact. Tricia cried out and gripped Royce's ass harder. There was no stopping the orgasm rolling over her, twisting her insides before flooding her body with the most intense pleasure she'd ever felt.

"That's it, sweetheart. Give it to me."

She had no choice but to give him what he demanded. Her body wasn't her own.

CHAPTER THIRTEEN

Anxiety crawled over Royce like roaches in the dark, making him twitch on the bench. The first inning had proved, unequivocally, Jason Holder's cure for a slump wasn't a cure at all. A person couldn't have better sex than Royce had experienced with Tricia the night before they left on the road trip, yet he'd given up three runs to a team he should have been able to best with his eyes closed.

Hell, maybe I should close my eyes. My pitching couldn't get any worse than it already is.

The Waves were using their best pitcher against the Mustangs in hopes of winning the first game of the series, and from the looks of it, their strategy would be successful. After two and two-thirds innings at bat, the Mustangs had yet to get a runner on base. Royce needed to keep them in the game by keeping the runs scored against them to a minimum. Before his divorce, the task wouldn't have been a problem. Hell, he'd struck out every player in the Waves lineup more than once in his years on the mound. That they were hitting his pitches like kids playing T-ball was depressing. He had to find his groove again, or he'd be picking splinters out of his ass in the Minor League.

"You okay?"

Royce kept his gaze fixed on the field. Bentley Randolph was one of the nicest guys on the team, but Royce wasn't in the mood for small talk. "Fine."

"Relax, man. You look like you're walking a tight rope without a net beneath you out there. Loosen up. This is a game, remember?"

Royce clenched his jaw tight, causing a nerve ending to fire in his neck. He reached up to massage the taut muscle. The left fielder smirked.

Turning his upper body toward his teammate because the pain in his neck wouldn't allow anything else, he asked, "What?"

"See? You're wired so tight, your own muscles are protesting. Do us all a favor and lighten up." At the sound of a bat hitting the ball, both men stood in time to see Tony Ramirez be thrown out at first base, ending the top half of the inning.

Fuck. Every inning the Mustangs didn't score meant added pressure for him to be his best. It had been so long since he'd seen his best, he could barely remember what it looked like. Grabbing their gloves, the two men walked out on the field together. As they approached the pitching mound, Bentley laid his glove on Royce's arm, silently asking for a second of his time. Turning, he raised an eyebrow in question.

"I know how outside stuff fucks with your head. Whatever it is you're strung out about, you'll get past it. Just remember, until you do"—he swept his arm out to encompass the field—"we've got your back."

After flashing Royce a brilliant smile guaranteed to make the sportscasters wonder what they'd been talking about, Randolph jogged out to his spot in the outfield and Royce stepped up to the mound.

For years, he'd suspected his teammate was gay, but two seasons ago when Sean Flannery joined the team at first base the attraction between the men had ended all speculation on Royce's part. Sean had since retired, and Royce still wasn't sure what the heck was going on between the two men.

It wasn't his business, he thought as he threw a warm-up pitch. He rolled his shoulders, letting out some of the tension he'd been holding in. The batter stepped into the box. Royce knew him. Batting eighth in the order, he had a low batting average and even lower on-base percentage. Like a fried chicken joint, Kiefer Reynolds had never seen an outside pitch he could pass up without trying to get a bite.

Jason flashed the sign Royce knew was coming. Why put fancy crystal on the table when paper plates would do?

Royce came to a set. He dropped his chin to his chest, felt for the seams of the ball until they lay against his fingers in a familiar pattern. Kicking his left leg high, he put all his strength behind the pitch. The ball sailed toward home plate, breaking low and outside at the last second. Reynolds swung and missed. *Strike one.*

Unable to believe he'd actually thrown a pitch that went where it was supposed to go, he turned to the scoreboard to verify the call. Yep. One strike on the batter. Maybe he still had it after all.

He took the sign from the catcher. Jason knew everything about every batter the Mustangs faced, so when he called for more of the same, Royce didn't dare argue. Going through the motions again, he found the seams and launched the ball. He'd done everything the same as before, but instead of breaking in front of home plate, the pitch remained on a straight trajectory—right down the middle of the plate.

He couldn't have served up a better pitch to hit if he'd tried. The sound of maple colliding with cow hide rang out louder than a church bell. He didn't even turn to watch where it went. That sound was unmistakable—he'd heard it enough in the last few months. The ball was gone. Taking a deep breath, he watched as the Waves' fourth run trotted across home plate.

Whatever he'd done right on the first pitch, he'd failed to

do on the second. And the worst thing was, he didn't have a fuckin' clue how the two pitches differed.

Tricia ignored the curses flying around the Mustangs' owner's private box. Though her heart ached for Royce, she was busy isolating the information from his last two pitches. Before the runner crossed home plate, she had the data sets side-by-side on her computer screen. They couldn't have been more different.

Excitement coursed through her veins. *Oh God! This is real! I have something to work with!*

Keeping one eye on the game, she fed the new information into the programs designed to analyze and quantify specific data. With a little luck, she'd have something to show Royce after the game, something he could use to fix what was wrong with his pitching.

While the programs ran in the background, she returned her attention to the data continuing to stream in. In the fourth inning, Royce struck out the lead-off batter with three beautiful pitches in a row, and a few Mustangs fans in the Waves stadium came to their feet to chant his nickname, "Strikeout! Strikeout!" After that, Royce seemed to get into a groove. He fell behind in the count less often, throwing more strikes than balls, but he was still allowing too many runners to get on base. Good defense by the other eight players on the field prevented the team from giving up even more runs.

Royce didn't come back out in the fifth inning, so Tricia packed up her computer and left the stadium. Though she was staying at the same hotel as the team, she hadn't traveled with them. Getting a cab outside the stadium was easy enough, and soon she was back in her room, her computer open, running every program she had to see what, if anything, could be gleaned from the new data she'd collected.

Something about the pitch sequence in the third inning bugged her. She'd been over it and over it, but every time she clicked away from it, she was drawn back to it, as if the data was trying to tell her something.

In an effort to see anything new, she isolated the data from the first pitch, bringing it up on her screen in every form available to her. A knock on her door drew her away. After receiving the pot of coffee she'd ordered from room service, she poured herself a cup then returned to the small desk where she'd set up her work. As soon as she sat down, one of the colorful graphs she'd seen a dozen times before caught her eye.

She blinked. Then blinked again.

I've seen that before. But when?

Setting her cup aside, she programmed a search for matching data. It wasn't long before an almost identical graph appeared on the screen.

Holy shit! It can't be.

Her hands trembled on the keyboard as she brought up the time stamp for the first data set. When it came up, she dropped back in her chair and stared at the information.

It is.

Oh. My. God.

Not believing what she was seeing, though down to her bones she knew it wasn't a mistake, she ran comparison programs on both sets of data. The similarities were there. Every muscle group she'd collected data from tonight in that instant when Royce threw his first perfect pitch was identical to the data she'd collected while she had been on her knees— sucking his cock.

It was impossible. But the data didn't lie.

Figuring out what it meant would be the hard part.

Royce obviously couldn't pitch with his dick in her mouth, so if the data was going to mean anything, she had to figure it out. And she would, as soon as she got a clue how to do it.

Staying away from Tricia slowly chipped away at his sanity.

The Mustangs were three games into a four game series with the Waves in San Diego, and Royce had only seen Tricia on the first day when she'd wired him up before the game. Staying away from her while they were on the road was killing him.

He'd pitched like crap the other day, but crap was one step up from shit, and he'd wanted to talk to her about his performance. He couldn't get her out of his head, and it had nothing to do with her research. If she'd discovered something that could help him she would let him know. He understood that. What he didn't understand was how she had come to mean so much to him in such a short period of time.

Sure, she was beautiful, and her brain was about the sexiest thing he'd ever encountered. He loved the way he could tell when she was over analyzing something. She'd get a crease between her eyebrows and she bit down on her lower lip. Fuck, that was hot, especially when he had his mouth on her pussy and she looked at him with that expression. She'd done it the other day when he had her in his bed, and he'd redoubled his efforts to short-circuit her brain. He'd done a pretty good job, if her orgasm was any indication.

Tony had told him she was working night and day to make sense of all the information she was gathering, and had asked to be left alone to do her analysis. In the meantime, with nothing to do since he wasn't due to pitch again until they arrived in Seattle later in the week, he had plenty of time to think about her.

Hell, when he wasn't obsessing about his dismal ERA, he was missing Tricia. He missed her voice. He missed her scent. She always smelled like spring—sort of flowery, but *warm* flowers. Fuck, he didn't know what he was thinking. Warm flowers? What kind of poetic shit was he coming up with? She smelled good, and God, she tasted even better. Thinking about her scent made him think about her pussy which rivaled every flower on the planet in beauty and scent.

Yeah, he had it bad, so when he saw her name on the Caller ID as he stepped off the bus delivering the team from the stadium, his cock was the first part of his anatomy to answer the call.

The first thing he noticed when she opened her hotel room door were her eyes. They were red-rimmed and swollen, but the flaw did nothing to detract from her beauty. Stepping inside, he closed the door then took her into his arms. She melted against him as if she'd held herself upright as long as possible, and once he was there, gave the duty over to him. A rush of tender possessiveness washed over him.

Always petite, tonight she seemed frail. Had she lost weight? Damn. He silently berated himself for not seeing to it she ate when she was working. From this moment forward, he'd look after her. "Did you have dinner?"

"No. Wait. What time is it?"

Shit. How many hours had she put in if she didn't know what time it was? "Close to midnight. Weren't you at the game tonight?"

She shook her head. "I told Tony to tell you I was going to stay here and work. I guess I lost track of time."

Being reminded of her work brought a now-familiar pang to his chest. He wanted her to succeed professionally, but at the same time he knew he couldn't let it happen. His duplicity was tearing him apart. "You're working too hard."

She didn't protest when he led her to the easy chair in the corner and urged her to sit. He placed a call to room service then returned to sit on the footstool in front of her.

"What's the rush? The data you've collected isn't going to morph into something different if it sits there for a few days…or weeks."

"I know, and I haven't been working on all the data, just a tiny part of it."

"Did you find something? Is that why you asked me to stop by?"

She rung her hands in her lap, and if she bit her lower lip any harder, it was going to need stitches. His gut twisted. She had found something, he just didn't know what.

"You can tell me. Is the program not working? You aren't getting the results you expected? What?"

"The program is working." She took a deep breath, raised her gaze to his. He fuckin' hated the pain he saw there.

"That's good, isn't it?"

"I suppose so, but I can't use the results. I'd be the laughing stock of academic research if I published my findings."

The thrill of victory coursing through his system was followed by a bitter rush of guilt. This was exactly what he'd hoped for. The best outcome he could imagine. She'd have the satisfaction of having accomplished something, yet no one but her would ever see it.

"Why not?"

She sighed, returning her gaze to her lap. He took her hands in his to keep her from wringing the skin off of them. When she tried to tug them loose, he held on tight. In some small way, he wanted to convey his support.

"Do you remember the first day you wore the wireless electrodes?"

Hell, yes. Of all the special days seared into his memory, that one was at the top of his remember-forever list. He was afraid he'd associate the smell of liquid hand soap with blow jobs for the rest of his days. "I remember. What about it?"

"I didn't shut down the program when...."

His blood turned to ice. His skin felt like ants were crawling all over him. Trying to process the implications of her words, he straightened. Her fingers slipped from his hands. She gathered them to her in a tight ball at her chest. The protective gesture nearly broke his heart. Withdrawing what little support his touch provided had hurt her.

"Tricia." He reached for her, but it was too late. She'd retreated into a shell he couldn't breach. "I'm sorry. Please. Tell me the rest."

In an attempt to convey his remorse, he laid his hands on her knees, and very slowly, stroked up and down her thighs. She remained silent, her chin tucked just above her hands, ignoring him.

A knock on the door startled them both.

"Room service."

Royce stood. "I'll get it."

CHAPTER FOURTEEN

After tipping the waiter, Royce lifted the cover from the plated food. "Looks good." Getting no response, he took the dish and returned to his place on the foot stool. He carefully spread a napkin in Tricia's lap then lifted a French fry to her lips. "Eat."

She swiveled her head, refusing to take the offered food.

Royce continued to wave the morsel under her nose. "Don't be stubborn. I said I was sorry. You have to eat." He decided to try another tack. "If you don't eat, I'm going to spank you."

She gave him a go-to-hell look then turned away. He thought for sure his suggestive comment would get her to take a bite.

He wasn't hungry, but he took a fry for himself, smacking his lips and moaning as if the fried potato strip was the best thing he'd ever eaten. "You don't know what you're missing. These are good."

Ah, at last. Acting like an idiot had done the trick. She faced him. He offered the snack again, and she opened her mouth to take it in. As she chewed, he brushed his thumb over her lower lip. "So beautiful." She was as wary as a lost kitten, but she allowed him to feed her. When most of the sandwich and fries were gone, she once again refused the bite he offered.

Royce returned the plate to the room service tray then resumed his place at her knees. "I'm listening. Tell me everything."

Tricia hugged her knees to her chest. She'd told Royce everything and he hadn't said a word. He'd just stood and started to pace, his bottom lip caught between his thumb and forefinger while he considered everything she'd said. At least he hadn't laughed. She wouldn't have blamed him if he had. She had a fit of hysterical laughter earlier—before she broke down and just plain bawled.

The whole situation was ludicrous. She had valid data that could possibly help Royce recover his pitching game, but there was no way in the world she could share the information with anyone—except him.

Chin resting on her knees, she tracked his methodical progress from one side of her small hotel room to the other. She loved to watch him walk. His long legs ate up the space with an innate grace that stirred her libido. He was like a caged animal—beautiful, sleek, and powerful. Too bad he wouldn't ever be hers. Her heart ached at the thought, but she wasn't stupid. They'd had fun together. Sex with him was the best she'd ever had, better than anything she'd ever imagined, but he'd never indicated he wanted anything more than a few hours of pleasure with her. Why would he? Women practically tripped over their tongues when they saw him. All he had to do was crook his finger and they'd follow him anywhere. He could have any woman he wanted, so why would he settle for a research scientist who couldn't remember her own name when he took his clothes off?

She didn't have a clue what he might be contemplating. Whatever it was, he'd be shocked to find out where her mind had gone since she'd shared her burden with him. While her brain came to terms with the fucked-up mess she called research, her body had moved on to more basic pursuits. Watching Royce pinch his lip made her nipples pucker and ache for the same attention. She could still feel his roughened fingertips on her breasts, teasing and tugging on the sensitive tips until she cried out. Then his soft lips and tongue soothed the pain away, creating a new, more urgent ache lower in her body.

It was all she could do to let him work through the impossible situation she'd thrown them both into when what she really wanted to do was jump his bones, drag him into bed, and let him do in-depth research on her body. In the name of science, she'd catalog every inch of his body as well. Something so exquisite deserved to be documented. Not a single thing she'd learned in her human anatomy classes had prepared her for a man like Royce. His muscles were individual works of art. Together, they were like a symphony orchestra, each instrument working in harmony with the others to create a unified composition that was more than the separate parts.

She was deep in her thoughts when he abruptly stopped and turned to her. The hairs on the back of her neck stood up. He'd tossed his suit jacket off when he began pacing. Standing there in his expensive dress shirt and slacks, his tie askew, shoulders back, hands loose on his hips, he looked like an advertisement for men's cologne. She could see the tag line— "Sexy. Successful. Sinfully Seductive. Real men wear *Testosterone*." If she could bottle Royce Stryker, she'd be the wealthiest woman on the planet. She had about as much chance of bottling his essence as she did succeeding with her current project. Nil.

His gaze was unwavering, making her feel like a bug under a microscope. She tried, but couldn't read anything in his expression. Her unease grew. Had he decided to tell team management she was a quack? A fraud? She wouldn't be the least surprised if he had. She'd called herself worse names in the last twenty-four hours.

"I get why you wouldn't want anyone to know how you

obtained the data. It wouldn't look good, for you or for me."

"My reputation as a researcher would be gone. Everything I've done up until now would be called into question, and no one in the scientific or academic world would ever want to hear from me again."

He nodded. "So, we won't tell. But if you have something to help me get back in the game, then I want to see it."

"Huh?"

Royce gestured toward her computer sitting on the small desk littered with papers. "Come on. It's getting late, and we have an afternoon game tomorrow. Show me what you've got."

After the game, the team would be on a plane to Seattle where they would play three games against the Anglers before heading back to Dallas, ending the longest road trip of the season.

Tricia unfolded from the chair. Unclear why he wanted to see the data, she felt she owed it to him to present her findings. It would be up to him what he did with them, if anything. She sat at the desk. Royce dragged the footstool over and sat beside her. He was so close, she could feel his hot breath on her arm. She clicked a few keys, bringing the isolated data sets up on screen.

He listened intently as she enumerated the main points. Occasionally, he'd nod in understanding. A few times he asked her to pause while he studied the charts and graphs. If he planned to rat her out to management, he was at least going to do it from a base of knowledge. She gave him credit for using his head.

"How am I supposed to translate all this stuff into actions?" He straightened, the movement putting distance between them that she needed in order to think straight. "I mean, I see what you're saying. There are definite similarities, but I don't see how I can pinpoint the exact moment in my pitch routine when I should do whatever it was I did."

He stood and paced away. Turning, he wiped a palm over his face. "This is hopeless. I'm never going to get my rhythm back."

Tricia froze. He wasn't interested in her findings in order to be well informed when he blew the whistle on her. He was interested because he wanted to get his game back! She'd already come to terms with the fact her research probably wasn't going to lead to any great discoveries, but if she could help Royce fix his pitching, then all the years she'd devoted to this project wouldn't have been for nothing.

"But you can!" She spun back around to the computer. He stood behind her, watching over her shoulder. "Look. I got the game tapes." A few key clicks and she had video of Royce pitching side-by-side on the screen with the isolated charts from the pitch and the corresponding blow job. She pointed to the exact moment she wanted him to see then set all three screen shots in motion. "There. Did you see it?"

"Run the sequence again." Damn. She might be right. Interested again, he sat on the footstool. He watched the simultaneous screens run through several times. "Can you advance it frame by frame? Slow it down?"

"Sure." The video ran again, slower, one frame at a time, the dual data streams keeping pace. It didn't make a lick of sense, but she was right. He did the same thing with his thighs when he threw a good pitch that he did when she blew him.

"Look at this." She clicked the keyboard. The good pitch video disappeared, replaced by one of him throwing the same pitch, but the results weren't anywhere near as good. "See the data stream?" She pointed to the one from the blow job, pointing out where it differed from the information gathered during the *bad* pitch.

"Which muscle group is that from?"

"Primarily the abductors and the femoral triangle." She rattled on in her uber-sexy brainiac way. He caught a few words like Fast-Twitch, Type II, femoral artery, and some others he'd at least heard before, but what they had to do with his pitching, he didn't have a fuckin' clue.

"Whoa." He caught her gesticulating hands in his. "Speak English, please." He tugged, pulling her to her feet. "I've got a better idea. Why don't you show me?"

"Show you?" He saw the instant her brain switched from academic researcher to woman. Her pupils dilated and her cheeks flushed with color. Oh yeah. She knew exactly what he was asking her to do. God, he loved an intelligent woman!

He pulled his tie loose and began unbuttoning his shirt. "You don't mind, do you? I'm just a simple sort of guy. The best way to get this through to me is with a hands-on demonstration." He removed his shirt and went to work on removing his slacks. "When you're done, I'll demonstrate my knowledge of the subject."

"How do you plan to do that?"

"You'll see." He toed his shoes off then let his pants drop to the floor. Before he tossed them on the heap of his other clothes, he took out his wallet. His emergency condom landed on the nightstand. "It will require you being naked."

Her lips quirked up on the corners. "I see." She reached for the hem of her T-shirt.

"Let me." It took all of two seconds to strip her bare. He wondered what her electrode sensors would make of his muscles now. He was hard as a rock in every place that counted—had been since she'd started spouting scientific jargon a few minutes ago.

He stretched out on the bed then reached for her. "I'm ready for my anatomy lesson, professor."

Lord, he turned her brain to mush! How was she supposed to remember one muscle from another when there were so many fabulous ones on display? Hers for the touching. She joined him on the bed.

"What do you want me to do?"

"Touch me, babe. Educate me." His words should have sounded corny, but he sounded dead serious instead.

"You really want to know?"

"I really do. All those names don't mean a thing to me. I'm more of a visual, or in this case, tactile learner. Go over all the technical stuff again, but touch each muscle as you do. That way, I can associate your touch with the area I need to concentrate on."

She remembered a girl she knew in grade school who had trouble remembering the alphabet. One day, her teacher had brought in a box full of plastic letters for them all to play with. Something about feeling the shape of the letters helped the girl recall them better. From then on, they always had tactile learning tools in their classroom to go along with their standard learning materials. Perhaps Royce *would* understand better if she touched him while she explained the role of each muscle group.

"I'll need you to take off your underwear."

He moved fast, removing the garment in the blink of an eye. "I'm all yours. Teach me a lesson."

His eyes twinkled, leaving no doubt as to his meaning. He was going to enjoy his anatomy lesson, but if she had her way, he would learn something, too. Whether he could use the information to improve his pitching, she had no idea. It was worth a try though.

"I need to be between your legs." She crawled over him, trying her best to avoid looking at his genitals. There was no doubt in her mind where this lesson would end up, but before it did, she had every intention of giving Royce a crash course in anatomy.

She laid her hands on his thighs, just above his knees. "All the muscles in your legs work together to move your body in the direction your brain tells it to go. After prolonged repetition, the conversation between your brain and your body becomes abbreviated. In other words, you don't consciously think about each tiny movement, you think in general, and your body responds. Sort of like the shortcut keys on a computer. One tap and a whole series of pre-programmed things take place."

"Muscle memory." He propped up on some pillows and crossed his arms behind his head, angling so he could see as well as feel.

"Exactly. Tense your legs."

The hills and valleys revealed when he contracted the muscles were enough to make her mouth water. He'd kept up with the shaving, making it easy to draw her index fingers along his smooth skin. This is the longest muscle in your body—the Sartorius. It attaches to the inside of your knee on this end. Her finger glided north, along the bulge of his rectus femoris. As she skimmed near his groin, he sucked in a ragged breath between his clenched teeth. "It connects up here."

She touched a place on his hip just above his tight butt. Dragging her finger back down to the top of his thigh, she drew an imaginary line. "It forms the lateral border for the femoral triangle right here."

He sat up straighter. "Femoral triangle. I've never heard of it."

"That's where your problem is." She traced another muscle with her finger. "This is the abductor longus. It forms the medial border of the triangle." Her index finger brushed his sac.

"Damn, woman. Keep it up and school's going to be over too soon."

"Sorry." None of her advanced anatomy classes had been anywhere near as fun as this was. Royce was really trying to focus, and she wanted him to, but torturing him was so much fun!

She opened her first two fingers into a V then, starting about a third of the way down his thigh, they spread out along the two muscles until her palm rested flat against his leg.

"It's a small area, as you can see. A ligament forms the top of the triangle." With her free hand, she traced the crease between his thigh and torso on his other leg, coming to a stop at the base of his cock.

"Fuck, Tricia." At the harsh curse, she glanced up. His lips were drawn into a tight line, and a fire blazed behind his narrowed eyes. She would have laughed at his discomfort if she hadn't felt the same.

"The femoral artery runs through the femoral triangle. When you're aroused, it carries lots of blood to this region of your body. I've never read any research on what happens to the other muscles in the region, but it stands to reason some of the extra blood flow is sent their way. After all, they're crucial during intercourse."

"And in pitching."

She had to give him credit. He wasn't letting his obvious need interfere with learning what he could. "Exactly. These two muscles, the Sartorius and the abductor longus, along with the rectus femoris all registered the same responses during both activities. The successful activities," she amended.

"And during the not-so-successful activities?"

"Well, you saw the data. They were underperforming."

"Are you saying I pitch better with a hard-on?"

"Did you have a hard-on when you made that good pitch?"

"No, I didn't."

"But, I'm betting the blood flow to those muscles was elevated." She sat back on her heels, her brow knitted in concentration while she stared at his groin.

He could practically see the wheels turning in her over-achieving brain. He'd always found intelligent women sexy. Mix in her hands skimming close to his engorged cock, and it was a wonder *his* brain was functioning at all—starved of oxygen the way it was. It was time for recess. "I'm not sure I understood everything you were showing me."

She shifted her gaze to his face. "Want me to repeat it?"

"No, Professor Reed." He brought his knees up, maneuvering around so he lay on his side next to her. "Lie down. Let me show you what I've learned. If I miss anything, feel free to correct me."

There it was. The moment he'd come to crave. The instant when her megawatt brain shifted from business to pleasure. The thought lines on her face smoothed out. Her pupils dilated, and her nipples became berries, ripe for the picking. He couldn't wait to eat his fill, but first, he had a test to take.

He helped her arrange the pillows behind her so she could

see what he was doing. The idea of her watching him touch her made his balls ache. He was going to take this slow tonight even if it killed him. When she was comfortable, he took his place between her legs, using his knees to spread her wide. Her pink folds glistened with moisture. He leaned in close, taking a whiff of her scent into his lungs.

"God, I love your pussy."

"Royce." His name sounded like a breathless plea coming from her lips. As much as he wanted to give them both what they wanted, he was determined to show her he'd been listening. And, if his touch drove her crazy, as hers had done to him, well, payback was a bitch.

"Shh. Pay attention, professor."

A very unladylike grunt told him she wasn't exactly on the same page with him. Nevertheless, he put his hands on her legs as she'd done to him. Slowly, he inched upward, until his thumbs brushed the inside of her thighs so close to her pussy he felt her heat.

"Let's see if I've got this right." By the time he'd repeated her anatomy lesson, practically word for word back to her, she was squirming, her hips rising from the bed in an invitation a dead man couldn't have refused. Bending over her, he flicked his tongue across one nipple then the other. She arched her back, offering her breasts to him. He gave them equal attention, licking, sucking, and nibbling until she writhed beneath him.

Her right nipple slipped from his lips with an audible *pop*. Tricia's sigh was part relief, part dismay. His touch turned her gray matter to gray goo, yet she craved the feel of his hands, his lips on her body. Erogenous zones were one of the things she'd studied in anatomy classes, but she was certain the scholars had it wrong. Where Royce was concerned, her entire body was an erogenous zone—one he was intent on exploring, inch by inch.

She cupped his head in her hands, and like the pointer on a Ouija board, it moved of its own volition, skimming her torso, stopping here and there for his lips and tongue to explore. When he finally reached her mound, her breath caught on a gasp. Before she could beg him to end her torture, he kissed her pussy.

Her own tongue darted out, wanting to mate with his as he stroked her lower lips then dove inside her channel. She couldn't stay still. She couldn't get close enough to his questing tongue or his lips which seemed to be everywhere, devouring her body, destroying her psyche as he'd already conquered her heart.

She was on the edge of release when he abruptly stopped, sending her body into a tailspin. Gripping his hair as hard as she could, she yanked. "Oh. My. God! Don't stop!"

He looked positively carnal, smiling up at her with his lips dark and swollen from kissing her pussy and his cheeks and chin glistening with her juices. "Trust me, sweetheart. We aren't finished."

"We better not be." Oh God, her pussy ached. She'd been so close to coming—then, nothing.

"Don't worry." He crawled up between her legs and reached over her. "We're going to finish this together."

She heard the crinkle of plastic packaging and realized why he'd stopped. Her empty channel clenched in anticipation of being filled. A moment later, the head of his cock nudged at her entrance.

"Relax, sweetheart. Let me in."

Tricia sighed and let her legs fall open as far as possible. He entered her with a slow, deliberate thrust, occupying her body and overwhelming her senses. She couldn't ignore the way his cock stretched her labia minor almost to the point of pain or the way his solid presence filled her, made her feel more than full—complete. For a long moment, he held himself in check, allowing her time to adjust, she supposed. After she'd stepped back from the urgent need to come, she was content to hold him inside her, to savor the wonder of connecting so intimately, so completely with another human being.

She understood the physiology of the act, but the

textbooks hadn't even tried to explain the emotional aspect of welcoming a man into a woman's body. Royce wasn't her first, but he was the only one who had made her feel as if she couldn't bear to end the connection when the act came to its inevitable conclusion. So, she wrapped her calves around his thighs, and did her best to keep him from moving.

"I've got to move, sweetheart. Just a little." He lay atop her, his forearms supporting a good portion of his weight.

"I don't want you to go."

"I'm not going anywhere." He flexed his hips, retreating until she could feel the tip stretching her entrance. "Not for a while." He filled her again. "Christ, you feel so good."

"So do you." She tried to move her hips, but his body pinned hers in place. "Do that again."

"Your wish is my command."

The rhythm he set was tortuously languid, but because of the pace, she reveled in his penetration and lamented every inch of his retreats.

"I've never felt anything like this before. You're incredible, sweetheart."

Her heart was too full, her body too filled with him, with her love for him. She answered him with a soft moan, and rising up, she placed a kiss on his shoulder. Whatever happened in the future, she'd always remember this night. She could almost believe he loved her as much as she loved him.

With patience only a saint or a trained athlete could muster, he brought her to the pinnacle of pleasure. She was lost in the sensations building inside her, stoked by his hands, roaming her body, his touch awakening every inch of her skin. When he took her breast into his mouth and gently bit down on her nipple, she tensed then flew apart.

"So beautiful," he said. Only then did he give into his needs, pumping into her with hard, determined thrusts that quickly brought him to orgasm.

Sweat created a sheen on his body she couldn't resist. Tricia rolled onto her side, facing him. "It's my turn to lick you all over, don't you think?" She bent her head and swiped her tongue across his chest.

He groaned then moved to his back beside her. "You don't play fair."

"I learned from the best." She flicked her tongue over his nipple.

"God, Tricia. You're killing me."

"It's a nice way to go, though. Isn't it?"

"Hell, yes. Lick me again, sweetheart."

CHAPTER FIFTEEN

Royce stepped onto the mound in the bottom of the first inning, acutely aware of his teammates on the field and in the dugout who counted on him. He was damn tired of letting them down. Dropping his chin to his chest, he closed his eyes and thought back to two nights ago when Tricia had done her best to educate him—her soft voice spouting scientific jargon while she destroyed his sanity one touch at a time. As difficult as it had been to concentrate on her words, he'd managed to hang onto a few of the pertinent points, questioning her later about them in detail.

Even she admitted her findings and theories were questionable at this point, given how she'd obtained the data they were based on, but the woman obviously knew her stuff, and he'd be stupid, and an ass, not to take her seriously. If he could translate her thoughts into actions, he might just get his game back. If and when he accomplished his goal, he'd figure out what to tell Doyle about the validity of Dr. Reed's research.

During pre-game warm-up, he hadn't tried to do the things she'd recommended. That time had been for warming up his muscles, getting loose. Facing his first batter, he opened his mind to the nuances of his body. He rolled his shoulders to ease the tension gathering there. The wireless electrodes stuck all over his skin were constant reminders Tricia was aware of every muscle movement he made. Just like this morning, when she'd wired him up and had him go through her checklist until the readings coming through matched the ones she felt certain would put him back in the game. It had taken hours, and he still wasn't sure he remembered everything. Hell, how could he? There were a million details to think about from his shoulders down to his ankles.

The opposing player settled into the batter's box. Royce waited for Jason's signal telling him which pitch to throw. Nodding to indicate he understood, he brought his hands together in front. He felt for the seams of the ball, found the grip he needed. Time wasn't his friend at this point. Twelve seconds could seem like an eternity, but right then his internal clock ticked the time away with the force of a sledgehammer on a gong—each one punctuating Tricia's instructions.

Shoulders.

Arms.

Abs.

Ass.

Thighs.

Calves.

Thighs.

Thighs.

Thighs.

He could almost feel the uncertainty pouring off his teammates scattered across the diamond. They stood behind him as they always had, offering their support while trying to hide the fact they were losing confidence in him with every lousy pitch he threw. Starting the game off with a solid strike would put everyone on the field at ease.

Leather scraping against his fingertips gave him a rush almost equal to the feel of a woman's skin beneath his hand. Callused though his fingers were, they were as sensitive as any of Tricia's sensors, providing a wealth of information his brain processed faster than the fastest hard drive. Speed. Trajectory. Spin. Distance.

All four needed to be perfect, or as near to perfect as possible. He knew the second the ball left his hand he'd failed. The trajectory was off. The pitch sailed wide of home plate. The batter, a veteran of the game, knew better than to swing.

Ball one.

Royce was enough of a veteran to realize he couldn't dwell on the failure. He had to throw another pitch. Had to make the next one count for more than the first. Moving forward was all he could do.

He took the sign. Nodded. The grip came automatically after years of working to perfect his game. And up until Hannah had left him, everything else about throwing had been equally as effortless. Sure, in tight situations he thought more about the mechanics, but day in and day out, he didn't need to think about what he was doing in order to make it happen. Much like riding a bike, once his legs learned the rhythm, it wasn't necessary to think about pushing the pedals.

Tricia's mantra ran through his head again, only this time, he forcefully stopped the repetitious thought in mid-recitation.

It wasn't working. He'd never put so much effort into thinking about a pitch in his life. He couldn't work this way. Every time he thought about what his muscles were doing, he wasn't thinking about pitching. He might not be the brightest bulb in the stadium lights, but he was smart enough to see he was wasting his time on Tricia's theory.

The pitch left his hand. Unlike the previous one, this one found the strike zone. Unfortunately, the batter knew a gift when he saw one. He cranked the bat through the zone— connected with the ball with a solid thwack that made Royce's heart skip a beat. He didn't want to look. Didn't want to watch, but he couldn't help himself. He turned to track the ball as it sailed over his head toward the center-field wall. When it began its decent, Royce breathed a sigh of relief. Tony Ramirez snagged the ball out of the air before it could hit the top of the wall, getting the out and saving a homerun.

The defense held solid, preventing any runs from scoring even though Royce gave up a single base hit to the third player in the Anglers' lineup. The fourth batter then hit a ground ball to short, setting up a double play to end the inning.

More than a little disgusted with his performance, Royce dropped his glove on the bench then headed toward the clubhouse door, announcing to no one in particular, "I gotta take a piss."

The comment was nothing more than an excuse to find some privacy so he could attempt to get his head screwed on right. Just out of sight, he stopped and leaned against the wall. He had a minute—two at best. The sound of footsteps approaching at a fast clip caught his attention. No one should be in that part of the stadium during a game—not even him. He straightened just as Tricia skidded around the corner and headed straight for him.

"Royce! Oh my God." She was panting as if she'd run all the way from the upper reaches of the stadium. "Hurry. Take your pants down."

Her hands were on his belt before his brain caught up with her words. "What the hell?"

"Humor me, okay?" She shoved his uniform down to his thighs then dropped to her knees.

"Tricia! Stop."

"No time. Listen."

Royce held the tail of his shirt out of the way so he could see what she was doing. She gripped the cap of a marking pen in her teeth, jerked the writing end free then proceeded to draw a line on his leg. "Here. Right here, Royce. All the other sensors have perfect readings."

She moved to the other leg where she sketched a couple of lines. "Concentrate on these two spots and only these two." After placing the flat of her tongue smack in the center of the two triangles she'd drawn, a reminder of the night before, she stood. "Pull your pants up and get back out there. Trust me. This will work."

He watched her sweet round ass disappear down the hallway while he righted his uniform. They might as well commit them to the same asylum because they were both insane. She'd taken a huge risk coming down to the clubhouse, and there weren't enough lawyers on the planet to help them if they'd been caught.

Taking the mound in the bottom of the second, Royce was surprised at how relaxed he felt. At the end of the previous inning he'd been ready to admit his career was over, but after talking with Tricia, he realized his performance in the first inning hadn't been as bad as he'd thought. He hadn't struck anyone out, but other than the one pitch Woodburn had hit out of the park, his other throws had been decent.

Reviewing the previous inning, he knew something had been different about his mechanics. They'd felt familiar. Comfortable. Perhaps all the work they'd done on muscle control had been worth it after all.

Thanks to some good hitting, the Mustangs had tied the game in the top of the second inning. In Royce's mind, he had a clean slate to work with. If he could prevent the Anglers from scoring, his team had a chance of winning. The Anglers' pitcher was good, but he was known to tire early, forcing the team to go to their bullpen, and everyone knew the Anglers' bullpen was the worst in the league.

Jason Holder took his position behind the plate. It didn't take much for Royce to imagine the two triangles drawn on his legs. Hell, he'd never forget how the lines came to be there or the feel of Tricia's tongue on his skin marking him in her own way. Concentrating on those muscle groups, he threw his first warm-up pitch.

Fuck! He knew it was good before the ball left his hand. The pitch landed in Jason's mitt with a solid thud that was music to Royce's ears. The two men locked gazes. From ninety feet away, he could see the surprise in the catcher's eyes.

Tamping down the elation coursing through his body, Royce caught the returned ball and went through the routine again.

Imagine.

Set.

Pitch.

Once again, the ball went exactly where he wanted it to go.

Instead of throwing the ball back to him, Jason walked out to the mound. "I don't know what you're doing, but keep doing it." With a big smile, he dropped the ball into Royce's glove and returned to his place behind home plate.

He finished his final warm-up throws, gaining confidence with each one. The first opponent stepped into the batter's box.

"Strike."

"Strike."

"Strike."

Nine perfect pitches in a row. He retired the side without a single batter putting lumber to leather. Royce smiled inside, but it was too soon to believe he'd made a complete comeback. He would face the top of the Anglers' batting order in the next inning. If he could get past them, he'd allow his elation to show on the outside.

He was aware of the quiet around him on the bench. Baseball players were a superstitious lot. His teammates would have plenty to say after the game, but they weren't about to risk breaking the spell he was under by congratulating him. It was just as well. His head spun from an adrenaline high, the likes of which he hadn't experienced in nearly a year. He couldn't wait to celebrate with Tricia.

He'd take her out some place nice for dinner then take her back to his hotel room and make love to her until he had to be back at the ballpark the next day. God, he couldn't wait to have her beneath him, to hear her call his name as she came.

"Royce! You're up." *Shit.* It was times like these he wished he was in the American League where pitchers didn't bat. He plunked his helmet on his head and grabbed his bat from the rack. Stepping into the on-deck circle, he checked out the situation. At bat, batting eighth in the order, Bentley Randolph swung at the first pitch and missed. The second pitch went wide for ball one, but the left fielder connected with the third pitch for a single.

Base runners were a good thing, and with no outs, no one would be disappointed if he didn't hit a homerun, at least not this early in the game. Moving Bentley into scoring position would be enough, especially with the top of the batting order coming up behind Royce. He was perfectly happy to let them do the heavy lifting.

He glanced to the dugout, received the go ahead to swing away then stepped into the box. While he found a good toehold in the dirt, he checked out the defense. Like most opponents, they didn't expect much from him. He'd never been a power hitter, and the Anglers knew it. The infielders were playing up, ready for a bunt, or an infield ground ball of some sort. If he could power the ball past the infield, preferably on the right side of the field, he'd avoid a double play and, if not get on base himself, at least move Bent one base closer to scoring.

Pitchers in the National League often made the mistake of underestimating their own kind, and the Anglers' hurler was no exception. Though Royce didn't connect with the first pitch, he recognized it for what it was—a half-hearted attempt. The man didn't expect Royce to hit, so he wasn't being as cautious as he would if he faced a more formidable opponent. He'd made the mistake a few times himself and learned a successful pitcher couldn't afford to be complacent. Every batter, no matter what the statisticians said about the man's abilities, could be dangerous. As Royce dug his toe of his lead foot into the dirt a second time, he hoped he would be the one to teach this pitcher that valuable lesson.

He fouled off two pitches before he found the one he'd been waiting for—a fast ball just over the outside edge of the plate. The hit wasn't pretty—it looped over the heads of the infielders but fell short of the outfielders who had been expecting a lazy fly ball. While the Anglers scrambled to field the ball, Bentley, running like the devil was on his heels, slid into third base. Royce made his best attempt to reach first, but running had never been his thing, and the center fielder's throw beat him to the bag.

His teammates clapped him on the shoulder as he walked through the dugout to stow his batting gear. With the short stop, Tanner Haversford up to bat, there was little doubt the Mustangs would at least score one run this inning.

Leaving the scoring in the hands of the men who did it best, Royce filled a cup with cold water from the insulated cooler in the corner then resumed his place on the bench. Once again in pitcher mode, the men surrounding him left him alone. Peace and satisfaction settled into his bones. The feeling had eluded him for months, making him feel like an outsider in a place he had always felt at home, and among people who were as much family as they were friends. It was good to be back.

He was still riding high after more interviews than he could count and accepting congratulations from his teammates when he was informed Hannah was waiting in the guest lounge. He rushed through his shower, dressing in record time. He couldn't imagine why she was here, unless something had happened to one of his family members. They all loved his ex-wife and kept in touch with her. If there was bad news to be delivered, and they couldn't come themselves, they'd send her. The knot of fear in his stomach turned to confusion when she greeted him with an exuberant smile.

Before he could stop her, she launched herself at him. "Royce!"

Her body pressed up against his was familiar, and at the same time felt all wrong. As gently as possible, he removed her arms from around his neck.

"Hannah." He set her on her feet. "What are you doing here?"

"I needed to see you." Once, those words would have been enough for him, but she hadn't needed to see him in over a year.

"I'll be back in Dallas in a couple of days. Couldn't you have waited until then?"

"Aren't you happy to see me?"

"When have I not been happy to see you?" He was being truthful, but he'd hoped to spend tonight with the woman who'd made his comeback possible. There was no hope for it, though. Hannah had come all this way for a reason. Her elation ebbed, replaced by a serious expression he'd seen too many times in the months leading up to their divorce.

"Can we go somewhere and talk?"

"I've got to go back to the hotel with the team."

"Can't you come with me? I have a rental car."

He didn't really want to be alone with his ex, but he sensed what she wanted from him was something he no longer wanted to give. A discussion away from the hotel where the team was staying would probably be for the best. "Let me tell Doyle I have a ride."

When had she become so clingy? Because she practically wrapped herself around him as they walked, he had little choice but to swing his arm around her waist as they made their way to the parking lot. Once they were on the road, he directed her to a family-style restaurant in the opposite direction from his downtown hotel.

"We could just go to your room and order room service if you're hungry."

"I have a connecting room this time," he countered. "No privacy to speak of, even with the doors closed between us." Not to mention, he had no intention of being in a room with Hannah and a bed. Rumors flew faster than fighter jets, and since he had his game back, he didn't need the media speculating it was due to him getting back together with his ex.

"My hotel, then."

Any question as to why she had come all this way to see him fled. In Dallas, she'd have no way to corner him in a room with a bed. He wasn't going to go to her place, and she couldn't get past the gate at his. He hated to play hardball with her, but she'd left him no choice. "No. Whatever you have to say to me will be said in a public place."

A few minutes later, she pulled into the parking lot and cut the engine. Royce unfastened his seat belt and reached for the door latch, but her hand on his left arm stayed him.

"I don't want to go inside." Once upon a time, the pout on her face would have swayed him to do anything to make her smile again, but now, it only made him angry.

Resigned to having it out with her in the car, he sat back in his seat. "What *do* you want?"

"I made a huge mistake, Royce. I never should have asked for a divorce."

Hope flared bright for a split second, the flame dying as quickly as it had sparked. A month ago—no, two weeks ago, he would have given just about anything to hear those words from Hannah's lips. But not now. It had taken a brainy scientist with a dream to show him what had really been wrong in his marriage. He and Hannah weren't suited to each other. The woman had no ambition. He'd convinced himself they'd grown apart, but the reality was, they'd never been all that great together in the first place. As far back as high school, he recalled always being in charge of their relationship. He'd been the one coaxing her to make good grades so she could go to college with him, but when he'd won an athletic scholarship, she'd gone along with him, only she never registered for classes.

He faced a truth he'd been unwilling to see in all the years they'd been together. Hannah was lazy. "Are you still taking classes?"

Her brows knitted as she processed the change of subject. "No. I couldn't decide what I wanted to major in."

There was no way he could suppress the sigh that carried over a year of guilt with it. His career hadn't held hers back.

She'd never had any intention of having a career of her own.

"I see." And he did—with startling clarity. Hannah was a taker. She'd taken nearly ten years of his life and a chunk of cash he'd given out of guilt during the divorce. "How bad is it?"

"How bad is what?"

"Never mind." He opened the door. The overhead light came on, casting Hannah's face in harsh shadow. She wasn't happy with him, but he'd grown used to the sentiment. "Your financial mess is no longer my problem."

He leaned back in before shutting the door. "We're through, Hannah. The divorce was final months ago." Giving the door a shove to close it, he strode to the front door of the restaurant. He'd have a cup of coffee while he waited for a cab to pick him up. With a little luck, Tricia would still be awake when he got back to the hotel. If not.... He smiled, thinking of ways he could wake her body and her mind.

CHAPTER SIXTEEN

Tricia squirmed in her seat. In the early innings, she'd been all nerves and barely able to sit still long enough to follow the data streaming in. Only her belief that today was the day Royce would find the groove he'd lost months ago kept her in her seat. He'd been so close in the first inning. Like planets aligning, she saw the graphs merge one by one until only two were left. He hadn't been maximizing his thigh muscles.

Now into the seventh inning, he had eight strikeouts and a total of two hits for the game. Knowing he was done and the manager would go to the bullpen for the final two innings, his teammates mobbed him as he returned to the dugout. While her laptop was powering down, she took the opportunity to wipe tears from her eyes as she bent to retrieve the old canvas tote she used as a computer bag.

The special pass hanging around her neck would allow her access to the lounge where family and invited friends gathered to wait for the players, but since Royce hadn't issued an invitation, she decided to wait for him near the staff exit. There was no need to hurry. After the game he'd just had, there were bound to be reporters lined up to interview him.

Realizing she hadn't eaten since early morning, Tricia stopped at one of the snack bars. The vendors had just quit serving beer a few minutes before she got in line, so she ordered a soda to go with her hot dog. Royce would probably want to celebrate with champagne anyway, so forgoing the beer was probably for the best. She found a high-top table where she could watch the remainder of the game on an overhead monitor. She wanted to smile, but kept her expression neutral as hometown fans began to stream out of the stadium after the Mustangs added two runs to their total in the top of the eighth inning, virtually assuring a win.

Almost giddy with excitement, she ordered popcorn and nibbled on it until the game ended. Only then did she make her way to the heart of the stadium to wait for Royce.

Tricia chose a spot off to the side of the player exit, close enough to make out the faces of the people leaving, but not so close Security would wonder who she was or why she was standing there. Fans weren't a problem as long as they kept their distance. One by one the Mustangs' players filed onto the bus waiting for them. When it pulled away, her heart sank. She'd missed him somehow. She was about to head to her rental she'd left in the adjacent parking lot when a familiar silhouette moved into the light.

Royce. Only he wasn't alone. He had his arm around the waist of a petite, dark-haired woman. Too young to be his mother, and from the way she clung to him, not a sister either. Tricia stepped back into the shadows so he wouldn't see her. The couple seemed oblivious to their surroundings. Nothing could have brought home the fact she'd meant nothing to Royce more than watching him give his undivided attention to another woman.

He had every right to celebrate with anyone he wanted. She told herself she was happy for Royce, and she was, but deep down inside, she felt as if he'd ripped her heart out and stomped on it.

He didn't need her anymore. It didn't take a neuroscientist

to figure out what that meant. She knew getting involved with any of her test subjects was wrong, but when it came to Royce Stryker, her body had overruled her brain.

She had no one to blame but herself. Everything that had happened between them was her fault, from the first blow job to the nights she'd spent in his bed. It wasn't his fault she'd given more than her body and asked nothing in return. He'd never offered more than physical release, and she'd been too weak to say no.

Tomorrow, she would be back in Dallas, reassessing her project, trying to find a reason to continue. She couldn't tell anyone about her success with Royce. Doing so would invite questions neither of them wanted to answer. No self-respecting researcher took advantage of a test subject the way she had, and Royce certainly didn't want to tell team management he'd been fucking her.

Fucking. The word was like a hammer, shattering her heart into a million pieces. She'd been nothing more than a willing body for his pleasure while she'd gone and fallen in love with him.

Tricia returned to the hotel, packed her things. She needed to put as much distance between her and Royce as possible, and do it quick.

The trip home seemed to take a lifetime. She watched reruns of the post-game interviews on the television in the airport. Royce's comeback was big news, even for the local reporters who lamented about it happening in their town, against their team. The national news outlets speculated on the Mustangs' chances at winning the pennant this season, one even going so far as to predict a trip to the World Series now that Strikeout was back in action.

Every time she saw his smiling face on the screen another piece of her shattered heart broke off. But as painful as it was to watch the coverage, she couldn't tear her eyes away. In a perfect world, she would have celebrated with him, and he would have told the world how her ground-breaking research saved his career. But this wasn't a perfect world.

She used to imagine what it would be like to have the eyes of the world on her, to be acclaimed as a shining star in the world of neuromuscular research. She'd wanted to rise to the top of her profession, but more importantly, she had wanted to help people.

Now, all she wanted was for Royce to hold her in his arms, to tell her she meant something to him. Something beyond a means to an end.

But that's all she was to him. He got what he wanted from her. He had his career back. He'd moved on, and so would she. It was time to see what, if anything, she could salvage from the data she'd gathered.

Arriving home in the wee hours of the morning, she texted Tony Ramirez to let him know she wouldn't be working with him until he returned to Dallas. She left off telling him she wasn't sure they would continue even then. What did she have anyway? After weeks of working with the two players, she had a success she couldn't tell anyone about and a briefcase full of charts and data on another player who seemed to be perfection on the field. There wasn't a scientific researcher in the world who would say she had enough to warrant continued study.

Where the fuck is she? Royce pounded on Tricia's hotel room door until a man in a neighboring room poked his head out and threatened to call security.

His life was back on track, and it was all because of Dr. Reed. Throughout the interviews following the game, he kept expecting her to show her face, but she never had. They'd discussed the reasons he couldn't acknowledge her part in his comeback, if he ever got there, but still, he thought she would have wanted to be there with him, to share the triumph. How he got there would have to be their secret, but he still wanted her there.

Backtracking to the lobby, he approached the front desk.

"I'm looking for Dr. Reed in room 1416. She's not answering her door." Royce drummed his fingers on the marble counter while the woman wearing a black hotel uniform and a brass pin that said, "Rhonda - Assistant Manager," typed. Stopped to read. Typed some more. Every passing minute was another he wasn't with Tricia.

"Dr. Reed checked out earlier this evening."

Panic gripped his gut. She had to be here. She had to be. He needed her. "There must be some mistake. We're here. The team is in town for three more days. Check again."

The woman shook her head. "There's no mistake, sir."

"Did she give a reason? Was there something wrong with her room? Maybe she went to a different hotel."

Rhonda's eyes shifted from side to side as she scanned the computer screen in front of her. "That doesn't appear to be the case, sir. No complaints were registered. Had there been a problem, we would have moved her to a different room."

"Then, where the fuck is she?" There weren't many people in the lobby, but it seemed every one of them froze at his outburst. Great. All he needed was for someone to post a video on the Internet of him going nuclear on a hapless hotel clerk hours after one of the best games of his career. He flattened his hands on the counter and stepped back an inch. Taking a deep breath then letting it out, he forced himself to appear calm on the outside. "I'm sorry. I was out of line. Please accept my apology."

He couldn't breathe. Acting like everything was fine when his insides were twisted in knots was going to asphyxiate him before he got back to his room. In the elevator, he closed his eyes and went through the mental exercises Tricia had taught him, only in reverse. He willed each muscle group to relax until the paralysis in his lungs eased. Making a scene in a five-star hotel in the middle of the night wouldn't help him find Tricia.

Back in his room, he dug around in his game bag for his cell phone. Maybe she'd left him a message explaining her disappearance. He stared at the blank screen. Nothing. No messages. No missed calls. He dialed her number, pacing the room while the signal bounced from tower to satellite to tower, trying to locate her phone. When the connection went straight to voicemail, he swore under his breath.

"Patricia. It's me, Royce. Where the…? Call me."

He chucked the phone at the bed. It bounced once before landing on the floor with a thud. She would call. She would explain herself. She had to. He was dying inside. If anything happened to her…. No. That didn't bear thinking about. It was late. She had simply changed hotels for whatever reason, and she'd be at the stadium tomorrow. He'd catch up with her then.

Suddenly, he was too tired to go on. The adrenaline he'd been running on had finally worked its way out of his system. He ached from head to toe—not an uncommon thing after hours of physical exertion followed by more time being the personality the media expected of him. Exhausted, he stripped and headed to the shower.

Hot water helped ease all the aches but one—the one he'd hoped to ease in Tricia's arms. He missed her with an intensity he wouldn't have thought possible. From the very first moment he met her, he'd told himself to stay away from her, but keeping his distance proved impossible. She was so damn sexy. He loved the dance of intelligence behind those blue eyes of hers, loved driving the brainy scientist to the point where she couldn't form coherent sentences. Yeah, he loved her body and her mind, but he loved her heart more.

Ah, fuck.

Royce braced his hands on the shower wall and dipped his head, letting the water stream over his head and down his back. His balls hung heavy between his legs like ballast for his engorged cock.

When had he fallen in love with Tricia?

He thought back to their first meeting and the way she'd teased him about his aversion to blood tests. She hadn't been intimidated or impressed by his status as a professional athlete. All she'd wanted from him had been his body. A groan rose from his chest. She'd gotten what she wanted. The stunt in the storage room, going down on her knees—she'd taken him by surprise then taken his clubhouse virginity.

Her passion for her job stuck a fork in his heart. When she'd explained about how her research could potentially help wounded soldiers and others with catastrophic injuries, he'd fallen hard.

Now that she'd accomplished her goal, gotten him back in the game, was she through with him? Had he been nothing more than a lab rat to her?

It wasn't possible. There had been more between them than great sex and research. The way she'd responded to his touch, trusted him, gave her body and her orgasms even when he behaved like an ass. He'd never forget the night he took her to his house and spanked her. Fuck, she'd been magnificent, and he hadn't done anything to deserve her trust.

What they had was real. He knew it, but did she? He'd never told her he loved her, and she hadn't said the words to him, though her actions indicated deeper feelings. He'd only known her a short time, but he knew she didn't sleep around. He hadn't been her first, but her passionate responses had been sweet, as if she were discovering the wonders of sex for the first time.

He'd been in a state of semi-arousal ever since she placed her lips against his thighs earlier. After the game, anticipation of spending the rest of the night buried deep inside her had run in the back of his mind, fueling his need to get through the interviews as quickly as possible. He couldn't deny his physical desire to be with her, not with his cock demanding attention, but besides his baser needs, he wanted to talk to her. He wanted to tell her how it felt to be back in the game, wanted to share his euphoria with the one person who knew what it had taken to get there. Tonight's success was as much hers as it was his, even if they couldn't tell anyone how it had come about.

Damn Hannah. If she hadn't waylaid him, he might have gotten back to the hotel in time to stop Tricia from leaving.

He'd talk to her tomorrow, but waiting wasn't going to work for him. He wanted to talk to her now—no, two hours ago—before his ex had waltzed in and stolen the glory from the evening.

But instead of holding Tricia in his arms, instead of kissing her, instead of sharing his triumph then making love to her, he was standing in a rapidly cooling shower, his hand wrapped around his dick, easing the pain the only way he could.

"Have you seen Dr. Reed?" Royce stopped Tony in the hallway outside the clubhouse door.

"Nah. I don't think she's here. She texted me last night, said she'd see me when we get back to Dallas." He waved Royce away from the doorway. "We need to talk."

He'd expected Tony to assume yesterday's comeback had something to do with Tricia's research, and he was prepared to lie through his teeth. The truth was, he wasn't sure how much her scientific theory had to do with him getting back on track and how much of it he could attribute to just being around her. Maybe what he'd needed wasn't practical analysis, but to find a woman with a mind of her own to challenge him.

Tricia had helped him in both respects, he supposed. But she couldn't do the same for every player. For her to be successful, her research had to stand alone, without emotional involvement. He had to convince Tony to continue in the program. He'd seen the two of them together. There were no sparks between them. The way it should be. It was just his fortune, good or bad that the two of them struck like flint from the very beginning.

"I know what you're thinking."

"Don't get me wrong, Strikeout. I'm as happy as anyone on the team to have you back, but if Dr. Reed had anything to do with it, then we have a problem."

"She didn't. Trust me. I've been in a funk, you know, since Hannah left me. It just took me a while to get my head screwed back on right."

The center fielder's gaze remained steady, as if deciding whether he believed Royce's story or not. He called on his years of appearing calm and cool under pressure to keep from squirming under his friend's scrutiny. "You wouldn't lie to protect her, would you, Royce?"

"Would you lie to protect Clare?"

Tony wasn't stupid. He understood where Royce was going, dodging the question with one of his own. "Like a rug, my friend. Like a rug."

"Then don't ask me again. In the meantime, you continue with the program. She might have something, but we'll never know if we pull the plug on her research now."

"I don't like it, but I'll let her put those things on me for a while longer so she can get the data she needs. To tell you the truth, I don't see how it will do any good."

"If you're asking me, you've got the wrong person. I majored in marketing. When she starts spouting scientific jargon, my eyes glaze over."

Tony laughed. "*My* eyes glaze over, *yours* dilate. Big words turn you on. Don't deny it. I've seen it."

Royce chuckled. "Can't deny she's sexy as hell." He pinned the bigger man with a death stare. "She's mine, and don't you forget it."

"Or what? You'll beat me up?" Tony's smile took the edge off his words.

"No, I'll tell Clare."

Hand over his heart as if he'd been mortally wounded, the center fielder staggered backward. "Ouch. You don't play fair, do you?"

"Not where Tricia is concerned. Keep your hands to yourself." He jabbed his index finger toward his teammate. "You've been warned."

"Okay, okay. I get the message. I'm in for now. Good game yesterday. I don't give a shit how it came about, as long as it did." With a wave, Tony headed toward the clubhouse door once more. "Gotta go. Some of us have to play *every* game."

Sitting in the bullpen with nothing to do but watch the game, Royce had plenty of time to think. After trying several times to call Tricia, and all the attempts going straight to voicemail, he gave up on trying to reach her by phone. He'd asked the few people who knew of her association with the team, and none of them had seen her. Her absence, along with the message she left for Tony, led him to believe she had returned to Dallas. But, why?

It was frustrating, thinking of her so far away, and he had no way to contact her. What was she thinking? Did she have data linking his recovery to her work, and if so, was it something she could make public?

He doubted anything had changed in that regard, so there was no need to tell her team management had sent him to spy on her. The less she knew about his double role, the better.

After yesterday's performance, he was certain it was only a matter of time before Doyle got around to asking him if Dr. Reed's research contributed to his comeback. Telling Doyle the truth wasn't an option. His best bet was to be noncommittal. He could say taking part in the project had forced him to pay attention to his mechanics, which was true, and as far as he was concerned, her project had little or no merit on a larger scale.

Throwing Tricia under the bus wasn't something he wanted to do, but he had little choice. Telling Doyle her research was worthless would do less harm than admitting his comeback was based on data collected while receiving a blow job. Either way, Tricia wasn't going to be happy about his report.

"Holy shit!" Jeff Holder jumped up. Royce, along with the other pitchers in the bullpen joined the Mustangs' closer at the fence. "Did you see that catch?"

CHAPTER SEVENTEEN

Royce was in time to see Ramirez pop to his feet and make a throw to home plate. The runner on third base tagged up on the fly ball then made a break for home plate. He'd seriously underestimated the center fielder's throwing ability. The player slid toward home. Jason fielded the perfect throw from his teammate, tagging the runner out smoothly.

Cheers rose all around him for the incredible double play to end the inning.

"Man, that guy is good."

"He's saved my ass a few times, too."

"Glad he's on our team now."

Comments and praise flew as the pitchers returned to their seats. Royce remained at the fence, watching Tony walk, not run, to the dugout. A trickle of unease ran along his spine. Had the man been injured making the play? Or was he just savoring the memory with a slow walk off the field? Ramirez was one of their best players, offensively and defensively. Taking him out of the lineup would hurt the team.

Tony's run-saving catch replayed on the jumbo screen. It

was one of those amazing plays sportscasters around the country would remark on for years to come, but if Tony was injured on the play, the price of the runs saved was way too high.

Royce's suspicions became certainty when a rookie, fresh up from the Minor League, stepped in to bat for Tony in the next inning. With a little luck, whatever was ailing the veteran player was something a good massage could cure, but Royce's gut told him otherwise. There had been something telling in the man's posture when he left the field earlier. The pitchers surrounding him were a quiet lot as they contemplated what losing Tony Ramirez meant to their individual Earned Run averages. The uninformed believed outfielders were nothing more than extras on the field, but every pitcher knew those three men were the last line of defense. Because they had so much ground to cover, outfielders had to be the fastest, and the strongest players on the team, and able to remain focused for nine innings while being far removed from most of the action.

Everyone, including Royce, glanced at Tony's locker as they filed into the clubhouse, following their win against the Anglers. Word had traveled fast once he'd left the game. He'd pulled something in his arm or shoulder. No one knew the details, but the news quelled the usual exuberance following a win. Conversations were hushed, smiles were rare and didn't make it to the eyes.

Royce had just slipped his suit coat on when Tony joined them in the locker room. He was still in uniform, minus his cleats and cap. A sling supported his right arm. Not good.

"Hey, man. What did you do?" He gestured to Tony's injured arm as everyone began to gather around their friend and teammate.

"I have no idea." Frustration laced the center fielder's words. "One minute I was fine, the next, I wasn't. Hurts like a son of a bitch, I can tell you that."

Condolences came from all around. "Thanks," he said, waving his good hand. "I'll know more once I see the doctors back home."

"You need help packing up?" Without waiting for an answer, Royce grabbed Tony's duffle bag from the top shelf and began stuffing things inside. The sooner they got Tony back to Dallas, the better.

"Hey, leave my civvies out. I still gotta get out of my uniform."

"They're sending you back tonight, aren't they?"

"Yeah. There's a car waiting to take me to the airport. Can you help me get out of this?" Tony made an awkward attempt to free himself from the sling. "I need a shower."

"Hold still and I'll help you. It's not as complicated as it looks." Royce eased the strap over his head. "Call Tricia when you get home. This is the kind of shit her program is supposed to help with, for real. It wouldn't hurt to consult with her."

"I was thinking the same thing. You know how I feel about her research, but I saw what she did for you. It made me stop and think."

"I'm not sure she did anything but help me get my head screwed on right, but your situation is different than mine. She might actually be able to help you."

"Why don't you come with me? You're supposed to go back tomorrow anyway, aren't you?"

"Yeah. I'm pitching the first game of our home stand." If he played his cards right, he'd have an excuse to see Tricia. "Take me with you when you see her."

Tony raised one eyebrow. "I thought you two were tight."

"Were. Past tense. She isn't answering my calls."

"I'm heading to the shower. If you can get a ticket on my flight, you can come along."

She hadn't expected the call in the middle of the night from Tony Ramirez. He was on his way back to Dallas to see a specialist, but he wanted to talk to her first. As she waited for him to arrive, she paced her small living room. With the team out of town, getting into the stadium would have been a challenge, so she'd invited him to her place instead.

Taking the red-eye from the West Coast, he was coming straight from the airport. While she waited, she put on a pot of coffee, as much for herself as for her early morning guest. She'd been up late, going over all the data she had from Tony, focusing specifically on the muscles in his right arm and shoulder area. According to him, the trainers and the doctor who traveled with the team didn't have a clue what was wrong. An MRI hadn't shown anything, yet his pain was real.

Her doorbell rang as she finished her first cup of the jolting brew. Setting her mug down on the short bar separating the kitchen from the living room, she made her way to the door.

Tony Ramirez was a big man. His shoulders and barrel chest filled her doorway, but she barely saw him. What captured her attention was the man standing beside him. Her heart kicked into an atypical rhythm that had nothing to do with the coffee she'd consumed and everything to do with finding Royce Stryker on her doorstep.

"Sorry to get you out of bed so early. Can we come in?"

Tricia mentally kicked herself for not taking more care with her appearance. After splashing cold water on her face, she'd pulled on a well-worn pair of sweatpants beneath the over-sized college T-shirt she used as a nightie. She ran a hand over her hair, wishing she'd done more than slap at it with a brush and corral it with an elastic band.

"Sure." She stepped back so the men could enter. Her place was adequate for one, but the two new arrivals seemed to take up all the available space in her living room. She closed the door then edged past them to the kitchen. "Coffee?"

"That'd be great," Tony said.

"If it's not any trouble," Royce added.

She grabbed her empty mug off the counter, took two more from the cabinet and filled them. "Here you go. Make yourself at home while I put on another pot. Can I get you anything else? I think I have some cookies or something."

She was rambling and she knew it, but seeing Royce in her apartment, just a few feet away from her bed had her nerves jumping. Her rational self knew the man was here to help his friend, not to see her. Her heart and her body wanted to believe otherwise, even though she'd seen him with another woman wrapped around him less than forty-eight hours ago.

"No. Don't go to any trouble on our account." Tony picked up one of the mugs and moved to the sofa, which looked ridiculously small once he'd sat.

"Coffee's good."

She risked a glance at Royce who remained standing while he sipped his coffee. If she reached out, she could touch him. "I'll just get another pot started, then."

Her hands shook as she measured the grounds into the paper filter. One of these days she planned to invest in one of the new style appliances you just popped a pod into. For once, she was grateful she hadn't replaced her old model. Going through all the steps bought her a few extra minutes to get her conflicting emotions under control. She filled the carafe with water and dumped it into the reservoir then hit the brew button. After wiping the counter where she'd spilled grounds, she folded the dish towel and hung it neatly over the edge of the sink.

"You done in there?"

Royce. She glanced up. Her gaze locked with his. She was tired, too tired to hide her feelings for the man, so she flicked her gaze to the other man in the room. "I saw your catch on the news. It was spectacular."

"Not if it ends my career."

Tricia sat on the sofa next to Tony. "What happened? Was it the catch? The hard landing? The throw?"

"I don't know. It could have been either, or some combination of all three. When I came up to throw, my arm felt fine, but adrenaline can mask a lot of symptoms. I certainly had the power to make the throw, but afterward...." He massaged his upper arm. "I felt this dull ache. It started near my shoulder then went all the way down to my elbow."

"How is it now?"

"My range of motion sucks. My arm still aches, but I'm not sure if it's because of the injury or from being immobilized for this long."

"You said the MRI didn't show anything."

"Nothing conclusive. They thought I'd torn something, but it wasn't evident. They took X-rays, too. No broken bones."

"What's the next step?"

"More doctors. More tests, I guess. I don't have a clue. That's why I'm here. You've got all the data from before. I was hoping you could hook me up again, gather some information on what's going on in there now. If I know what's wrong, I can fix it. Right?"

"That's the theory."

"Then let's give it a try. You fixed Strikeout, you can fix me."

She dipped her chin to keep either man from seeing the heat creeping into her cheeks. "If he said I fixed him, he lied. He did it all on his own."

"We both know I couldn't have done it without you." Royce stood over them.

The crisp creases in his slacks reminded her of the night she'd knelt at his feet. He'd done wicked, wonderful things to her—things she would never forget. Her clit throbbed with remembered ecstasy.

"I understand why you might think your work didn't help me, but can we agree to disagree for now? All Tony wants you to do is see if your fancy program can detect what's wrong. If he can point the doctors in the right direction, then they can decide on a course of action."

Muffled music broke the tension. Tony stood, pulling a cell phone from his pants pocket. "Clare. I forgot to call her when we landed." Moving toward the kitchen, he raised the phone to his ear. "Hi, babe. Sorry, I forgot to call."

Deciding the only way to afford Tony any privacy in her small place, she looked up, intent on engaging Royce in conversation. His smile wasn't a happy one. "I'm sorry I barged in on you this morning. Tony didn't want to make the trip alone."

"You're a good friend to come with him, but won't the team miss you?"

"I was supposed to fly home tomorrow…today…anyway. I'm scheduled to pitch tomorrow."

"I never knew pitchers got special treatment."

"Didn't you?" This time, his smile was downright wicked. "You certainly know how to make a pitcher feel special."

Tricia darted a glance toward the man in the kitchen. "Royce!" she hissed.

"Don't worry. He might suspect, but he doesn't know anything for sure, and if he did, he'd keep his mouth shut. If you had any idea the shit Tony has done, you'd faint dead away."

"What kind of sh…stuff?"

He held a hand up. "Not my story to tell."

Tony walked back into the living room. "That was Clare, my wife. I told her she could come over. I hope that's okay?"

Oh Lord. "I should put on some clothes." She stood.

"You look fine," Tony said. "Can you just hook me up, run the tests?"

"Let me get presentable." No way was she letting the wife of a Major League Baseball player catch her in sweatpants and a sleep shirt. It was bad enough Royce and Tony had seen her at her worst. She made a quick dash for the bedroom, shutting the door behind her.

Standing in the tiny walk-in closet, she stripped to her panties. She had just fastened her bra when her bedroom door opened. The closet door swung outward, and since she lived alone, she kept it propped open with a brick. With nothing between her and whichever man was in her bedroom, she grabbed for the first thing she could get her hands on.

Royce filled the doorway. Her foolish heart did a flip-flop before she remembered he wasn't hers. Whatever reason he had for cornering her, it wasn't the reason she hoped it was. It never would be.

"Nice shirt." His gaze tracked downward. The corners of his mouth lifted in a genuine smile.

Gripping the hanger in a tight fist, she let her hand drop to her side. What difference could a shirt make? He'd seen more of her than was revealed by her bra and panties. "What do you want?"

"To thank you for what you did for me, and to tell you, you didn't have to leave. I wasn't going to tell the press about us."

If he'd thrown a fastball at her heart, he couldn't have wounded her any deeper. She'd done nothing but think about what happened between them since she left Seattle. He had no way of knowing she'd seen him after the game with another woman, and she wasn't going to tell him. Let him think what he would about her reasons for leaving. He was partially correct in his assumptions. She had fled for the reasons he stated, among others he'd never know. He'd clearly moved on, and she'd been afraid he would tell the world what a fraud she was. But before her plane touched down in Dallas, she'd come to another conclusion, one she suspected was the real reason she'd run away in the night. She'd fallen completely in love with Royce. If she'd needed proof her feelings weren't returned, she'd gotten it in that touching scene in the parking lot after the game.

She'd been stupid to think there was anything between them. He'd never said he loved her, so she couldn't expect him to suddenly declare his undying devotion to the world.

"I didn't do anything…." She cut herself off before the words, *but love you*, spilled out. "You worked it out on your own."

"We both know what really happened, and I'm grateful. I just wanted you to know I'll never forget what you did for me."

Grateful. The word would have been a validation coming from anyone else, but from Royce, it made her feel cheap. The doorbell sounded, and they both looked in the direction of the living room.

"That was fast." Tricia assessed the shirt she still held. A basic pullover style, it would do for now. She yanked it off the hanger. "Tell them I'll be out in a minute."

Instead of taking the hint, he took another step inside the closet. "I looked for you after the game. Why did you leave?"

She almost choked on the hysterical laughter trying to bubble out of her throat. Of all the things she thought he would say, she never thought he would lie to her. "I don't want to talk about it. Not now, not ever."

His gaze raked over her face, searching for a crack in her armor, she supposed. He must not have found what he was looking for because he took a step back.

With a silent nod, he exited the closet. Once she heard the bedroom door open and close, she grabbed for the clothes rod to steady herself. Her knees were weak, and her heart was racing. How many times could a heart be trampled on before it broke beyond repair?

Fuck! Royce pasted on a smile for the newcomer. He'd just left the woman he loved standing half naked in a closet for no good reason he could think of. As Tony introduced him to his wife, Royce went over all the ways he'd messed up with Tricia. The list seemed endless, but at the top was the fact he hadn't told her he loved her.

He'd had every intention of saying the words to her a minute ago, but her cold reception had iced that idea. Besides, a woman deserved better than to hear those words spoken for the first time in a cluttered closet while strangers occupied her living room. Still, the words had nearly burned his lips, wanting to be out in the open.

While Tony and Clare enjoyed a sappy reunion he wouldn't have thought possible for the Mustangs' burly center fielder, Royce rummaged around in Tricia's kitchen. He found another coffee mug in the cabinet nearest the sink. After filling it for Tony's wife, he slid it across the counter. "Coffee, Clare?"

"Thanks." The couple broke apart. Tony brought his mug to the kitchen for a refill while his wife sipped from her cup.

"Nice game the other day."

"You watched?" He refilled his and Tony's mugs then leaned against the far counter, coffee in hand.

"I watch every game. I even DVR the ones I have to miss and watch them later."

"You must have been crazy when you saw Tony get hurt."

Her expression grew serious. "Crazy doesn't even come close. If I could have leapt through the television set to be with him, I would have." She snuggled up close to her husband's uninjured side. He slid his good arm around her waist, pulling her closer. "I hope Dr. Reed can help him. The game means so much to him."

"You think she can?" The hope in his teammate's voice was evident.

"Maybe." He'd been debating with himself all the way from Seattle over what, if anything, he should tell Tony about how Tricia had helped him. "Off the record?"

They both nodded, and Royce continued. "Without her, I wouldn't be back in the game. She'll tell you she didn't do anything, but she isn't being entirely truthful. The data she collected played a huge part in my comeback. However, there are aspects, details that will remain private. I don't know if she can help you, but I believe in her work. I think it has enormous potential."

"I knew you were hiding something, Strikeout."

"Only to protect her. Her work is important. It doesn't deserve to be ridiculed because of what happened between us."

"I figured out you guys were in love with each other a long time ago. I can see how a personal relationship might compromise her research. That being said, I'm not a scientific scholar. I don't give a flying fuck about propriety or conflict of interest. I just need to fix my arm, and fast. The lady doctor can be as inappropriate with me as she needs to be as long as it helps get me back on the field."

"Hey!" Clare gave her husband a playful punch in the gut. "All inappropriate behavior gets cleared through me. Okay?"

Tony's smile for his wife was tender. "Always, my queen.

Always."

Tricia's reemergence from the bedroom spared Royce from witnessing another PDA from the loving couple.

"Good morning." Tricia scooted past the entwined couple to join Royce in the kitchen. Introductions were made then she refilled her coffee mug and took a sip. She was sunshine fresh in white denim jean shorts and the yellow top she'd been clutching to her chest when he walked in on her. Her hair was in a clip at her nape and her feet were bare. He wrapped his hands tight around his coffee mug to keep from touching her. He seriously doubted Mr. and Mrs. Ramirez would mind if he fucked Tricia on the kitchen counter in front of them, given the stories he'd heard about the couple, but he couldn't say the same for Tricia.

"What a lovely necklace." Tricia went up on tiptoe and leaned across the counter to admire the gold and diamond bauble around Clare's neck.

Royce went hard as stone at the sight of Tricia's ass pointed in his direction.

"It's very special to me," the other woman said. "I'm never without it."

"I've never seen anything like it. Where did you get it?"

He had to do something to get Tricia off the subject of Clare's necklace. If the rumors he'd heard were true, that was a conversation he didn't want to be a part of. Royce opened the refrigerator and peered inside. "You have anything to eat in here? I'm starving."

Tricia turned to look at him. "Not much. Eggs. Bread. Cheese. Basics."

"Anyone want breakfast?"

"Yes." All three answered in unison.

Royce chuckled. "Why don't we try the chorus again? I think a couple of you were off key."

"Shut the fuck up and cook, Strikeout. We haven't got all day, and Dr. Reed needs to take a look at my arm."

"Okay, okay. But no complaints." He pulled the egg tray out and set it on the counter.

"I can help," Clare said.

He was grateful for Clare's offer since he knew less than nothing about cooking. He'd learned enough by trial and error to get by since Hannah left him, but no one would call him a chef. Tony's wife took charge, assigning him easy tasks that allowed him to keep an eye on the other couple. Tony had stripped off his shirt, and Tricia was busy applying the wired electrodes to his upper body.

He snuck a glance at the woman beside him. She was busy stirring the scrambled eggs and didn't seem in the least bit fazed by what was going on in the other room. He wished he could be as calm. For Tricia, the procedure was nothing more than a science experiment, but Royce's gut twisted at the sight of her hands on another man.

The woman had brought him back to life in more ways than one, and he was going to win her over, some way, somehow.

CHAPTER EIGHTEEN

Tricia focused on the man in front of her. What had occurred between her and Royce was best forgotten. She had to admit, it meant a lot he hadn't discouraged Tony from coming to her for help. He'd said he believed her work played a part in his recovery. Just because he couldn't tell the world how she'd helped him didn't mean he wasn't sincere.

She attached the last wire then plugged the ends into the box that would translate the electrical impulses into quantifiable data. Turning to her subject, she waved a hand at the box. "All set."

Tony held his right forearm cradled to his chest, supporting his injured limb without the sling he'd been wearing when he arrived.

"This is going to be painful, but can you let your arm hang naturally to your side?"

A light sheen of sweat coated Tony's face by the time she had put him through the same routine she'd used to gather his baseline data.

"I've got enough for now," she said, disconnecting the

wires from the box. She helped him put the sling back on, leaving the electrodes attached for the time being. "Let's eat. Afterward, I'll take a look at the data, make sure I have good readings. If so, then you can go. It'll take me a while to run the comparisons."

Clare insisted on cleaning the kitchen before she and Tony left for his appointment with the medical staff at the stadium. Tricia thanked the woman then got to work on the new data sets. She was so absorbed in her analysis she didn't look up until she heard her front door close. She blinked to refocus her eyes. Everyone had gone except Royce.

"Aren't you going with them?"

"No. I said I'd stay behind. If you find anything, Tony wants you to bring it over to the stadium. With everyone still out of town, security wouldn't let you in by yourself."

He was right. Her pass was only good when the team was in town. If she wanted in the stadium, she'd need him to escort her in. "Thanks. You've got to be tired. Why don't you go home, get some rest? I'll call if I need you…I mean, if I want to go to the stadium."

Much to her dismay, the man kicked off his shoes and stretched out on her sofa. "No car. We took a limo from the airport."

"My keys are on the table by the door. I won't be going anywhere." Having him this close, being alone with him was wreaking havoc with her body systems. She didn't have time to deal with any of the malfunctions going on. Not the ache to have him inside her. Not the pain of knowing he would never be hers. Not the hollow feeling where her heart was supposed to be. Not the eat-gallons-of-ice cream despair weighing her down.

"I didn't get much sleep on the plane. None, in fact. Tony complained the whole way. You've never experienced pain until you've heard about it in three languages. Did you know he speaks Spanish and Italian?" Royce punched one of her throw pillows then rolled to his side facing away from her. "Wake me up when you're ready to go."

Not if. When. Did he really have so much confidence in her? That would make exactly one person who did since she was fresh out of the commodity herself.

She opened her mouth to say he might be more comfortable on her bed, but thought better of it before the words left her mouth. She'd never be able to sleep there again for imagining him naked in her bed. He might be snoring on her sofa, but he was doing it with his clothes on. She could live with those memories. Barely.

Ignoring his presence as much as she was capable of, she returned her attention to Tony's situation. Crunching the new data took the most time. From there, it was fairly simple to compare and contrast the information with the previous readings.

A buzzing noise dragged her attention away from the computer screen. She searched around for her cell phone, found it in her purse by the door, and quickly concluded the sound had come from another device. The buzzing started up again. She followed the sound to Royce's suit coat draped over a chair at her small dining set. *Probably his new lover.*

Retrieving the phone, she clutched it in her hand and crossed the room, debating whether to wake up its owner or not.

"What?" Royce rolled to his back. He looked confused and rumpled, but it took only a moment for his brain to put the pieces together. He sat up, running a hand over his face and through his hair.

"Your phone. Someone was calling you. I thought it might be important."

He took the item in question from her outstretched hand, tapped the screen a few times then said, "Tony," by way of explanation. He punched the screen again and a ring tone filled the room. After two rings, a man's voice came over the line.

"Strikeout. How's it going over there?"

Royce looked to her for the answer. "Hi, Tony. Dr. Reed here. I've been studying the data, and I can't find anything wrong. I don't know what to tell you." She'd been going cross-eyed looking at the charts and graphs. She'd even created a new set, certain she had done something wrong the first time. The man's pain was coming from somewhere, but the data revealed nothing. She felt less than useless.

"Look, they're talking about surgery over here. They think something is torn. Please tell me you have something to keep me from going under the knife. I'd be out the rest of the season with no guarantee of coming back—ever."

The desperation in Tony's voice was evident. He was grasping at straws, and she couldn't blame him. The graphs she had memorized flashed through her brain. "Tony. I can't say for certain there isn't a tear, but all my data suggests there isn't one. So did the MRI you had yesterday. The only thing I've seen even remotely out of sync is a twitch below your right shoulder blade. It could be a pinched nerve. If that's the case, I'd suggest you see a chiropractor instead of a surgeon."

Silence reigned on both sides of the connection.

She shifted from one foot to the other. Royce's steady gaze and quiet smile boosted her confidence. "What can it hurt? If it doesn't work, surgery will still be an option."

"We have a chiropractor here. He wants to talk to you. Can you come down?"

Royce nodded, already slipping his feet back into his shoes.

"I'll be there as soon as I can."

"Thanks, Tricia. Tell Strikeout to drive careful. You're the only thing standing between me and a scalpel."

"I'm right here, Ramirez. I can hear you."

"I meant for you to hear me. Get her here in one piece, or I'll take you apart with my bare hands."

"And I'll help him." Tricia smiled at Clare's comment.

"On our way." Royce ended the call. "What do you need to take with you?"

Tricia glanced at the papers scattered over her desk. "My computer and all the papers." She powered down the computer while Royce gathered and stacked the reports she'd printed out.

"Looks like you've been busy."

"You slept for nearly three hours." He'd said he hadn't slept much on the plane, and having seen him leave the stadium the previous night, she doubted he got much sleep then, either. Forcing those thoughts from her head, she took the stack from his hands and stuffed them in the bag with her computer. "Let me get some shoes. I'll sort the paper on the way."

Once they were in her car on the way to the stadium, she had a chance to think about what they were doing. "I'm not making any promises. There could be a glitch with the data."

"Or not." Royce glanced her way before returning his eyes to the road. "What do you think? Is there something wonky with the data?"

She shook her head. "No. I don't think there is."

"Then go in there and tell Dr. Stephens. He's the chiropractor the team keeps on retainer. He consults on most injuries. I've always thought he seemed like a reasonable kind of guy." He nodded toward the bag she held in her lap. "Get your ducks in a row, then. These people are all about facts."

"The data doesn't lie," she told the assemblage of medical professionals gathered around to hear what she had to say. "As you can see by comparing two data sets, all the muscles in his arm and shoulder are functioning at relatively the same capacity they were three weeks ago when I took the baseline readings. His range of motion is limited at this time by the pain he's experiencing, nothing more. Once the cause of the pain is removed, he should be one-hundred percent again."

She wished she'd taken time to change her clothes. Nothing screamed airhead like a blonde in shorts and sandals. At least she had her fuck-you-I-have-more-advanced-degrees-than-you-do voice at her command at all times. If nothing else, using it made her feel more in control than she was.

Because of their numbers, they'd borrowed Doyle Walker's office for their meeting. A couple of the men sat together at one of the conversation groupings, comparing the data sheets she'd brought. The rest watched her as if she might abscond with their would-be patient if they took their eyes off her for a second. The tension in the room was thicker than mucus and just as pleasant.

Tony, one arm in a sling and the other wrapped around his wife's shoulders, gave her a weak smile from their place on the sofa. She smiled back, wishing for his sake she had more than a hunch to go on. She'd be more confident of her position if the medical professionals had consented to let her see the X-rays and MRI results, but no amount of pleading on her part or Tony's had convinced them to open their tight fists. They didn't trust her, and they sure as hell didn't respect her.

To distract herself, Tricia let her gaze wander over the artifacts and treasures in the team manager's office. Photographs and plaques covered the walls. A bookshelf doubled as a trophy case on the wall nearest the desk. A bowl filled with used baseballs sat front and center on the coffee table before her. She picked up one of the balls and examined the writing scribbled on one side.

"Jason Holder's walk-off homer from the National League playoffs last year." The last time she'd noted Royce's location, he'd been looking out the massive window that formed the back wall of the office and provided a spectacular view of the field below. Having him so close made her nervous. She put the ball back in the bowl and picked up another.

"Let me see that." He reached over her shoulder. She almost dropped the ball when their fingers brushed as they passed it between them. Maybe being disgraced as a researcher wouldn't be so bad after all if it meant never having to be this close to Royce again. She didn't know how much more torture she could take.

"Shit. What's this doing in here?"

"What is it?" Tony asked.

Royce held the ball up. "It's the ball Suzuki hit off me two years ago."

"The one that went into orbit?"

"It didn't leave the atmosphere, asshole."

Tony laughed at Royce's piqued retort. "Close enough. I wouldn't be surprised if it was recovered by a satellite."

Royce came around her chair to place the ball back in the bowl. He picked up another and examined the writing on it. "Wonder if he has any of your hits in here?" He examined a few more. "Doesn't appear so. Interesting, don't you think?"

"Keep looking, Strikeout." Everyone turned toward the booming voice. Doyle Walker stood in the open door, surveying the assembled group. "There's at least one in there." Advancing into the room, he shut the heavy wooden door behind him. "Someone want to tell me what's going on?"

"The quacks want to cut me open in order to fix something they admit they aren't sure is even there." Tony got to his feet. "Dr. Reed thinks differently. I'm inclined to agree with her."

Doyle listened—nodded—then directed his attention to the huddle of doctors. "Is that true?"

"We think exploratory surgery is the best option." Tricia frowned at the famed doctor's declaration.

The manager didn't agree or disagree. Instead, he focused on her. "What do you recommend?"

Tricia stood, clasping her hands together in front of her to keep them from shaking. "Based on my research, I think it's nothing more than a pinched nerve. Most likely, a session with a good chiropractor could alleviate the pain and get Mr. Ramirez back on the field for tomorrow's game."

"I opt for door number two, Tricia...I mean, Dr. Reed's solution."

"Your opinion is duly noted." Doyle turned to Royce. "You've had ample time to assess Dr. Reed's work. I guess now is as good a time as any for your report. What's your opinion on Dr. Reed's project? Should we listen to what she has to say or not?"

Tricia swayed, the blood draining from her head to pool in her feet. *Report? What did he mean by that?* Her eyes darted to Royce. The apologetic expression on his face confirmed his duplicity. He'd been sent to spy on her and report back to team management on the validity of her project. He'd have no choice but to throw her under the bus. She sank into the chair behind her and braced for the impact.

Fuck and double fuck!
The color drained from Tricia's face and for a second Royce thought she might faint. God, he was an asshole for putting her through this. He'd hoped to find a time to speak with Doyle privately, to set the man straight. There was no reason for her to know he'd been gathering intelligence for team management regarding her research. No way was he going to give specifics about what had occurred between them, but he could be truthful without details. As she collapsed, obviously expecting the worst, he prayed he still had a chance with her once he said his piece.

"You all saw the game the other day. I think Dr. Reed's research speaks for itself. I've been struggling for months. I don't know how much of my problem was in my head and how much was physical, but Dr. Reed pointed out issues I was having with certain muscle groups. By paying attention to those, I was able to bring my game around. I don't think I could have done it without her."

"Besides," he continued. "What's the harm in trying what she suggests? It's a chiropractor for Christ's sake not a Voodoo ceremony. The way I see it, Ramirez hasn't got anything to lose. If it doesn't work, surgery would still be an option."

"My thoughts, exactly." Tony added his opinion. "It's my body. I vote for the chiropractor."

"But—"

"The chiropractor it is." Doyle's decision cut off the team doctor's protest. "Everybody clear out."

He made shooing motions, and they all made their way to the door. "Ramirez." Everyone, including Tony, stopped and waited to hear what the man had to say. "Let me know how it goes."

"Yes, sir."

They turned as one and filed out the door. Royce breathed a sigh of relief. Doyle hadn't pressed for a detailed explanation, and had still gone with Tricia's recommendation. He hoped like hell she would give him time to explain. The first to arrive at the elevator filled the car, leaving Royce and Tricia, along with one of the trainers to wait for the next car to take them down to the bowels of the stadium.

"I hope you're right." The older man spoke. It was common knowledge Herschel Ford had been with the team ever since they moved to Dallas from Washington, D.C. decades ago. "I don't want to see Tony out for the rest of the season, especially now that we've got Strikeout back in action. We might still have a shot at the pennant."

"I wouldn't be back if it weren't for Dr. Reed."

Tricia's glare told him to keep his mouth shut, but he couldn't. If there was anyone on the wellness staff with the ability to influence the opinions of the others, it was Herschel. "You should take a look at the research she's doing. Even if this doesn't work out with Tony, there's no doubt in my mind it could one day change the way we do physical therapy."

"Really?" The elevator dinged, and they all stepped inside. "You're that confident in her research?"

He'd done what he wanted, planted a seed of interest in the man's mind. "I am. When Doyle asked me to take part in the study, he had some concerns about the possible use of the information, so he asked me to be his ears and eyes on the program. I found nothing to be concerned about." He glanced at Tricia. Facing forward, her gaze glued to the red numbers overhead, displaying the floor numbers as we descended from the uppermost level to the lowest, she appeared uninterested in the conversation. He hoped she was paying attention because he was sure he'd never get another chance to tell his side of the story. This was as good as it was going to get.

"I don't know the full scope of what her program can do, but I feel this kind of technology is the future of rehab and physical therapy." They'd reached the lower level. The elevator doors opened with a *swoosh*. Royce put his arm out to hold the door open while they exited the car.

"It's interesting to hear your opinion, Strikeout," Herschel spoke as he left the car. "I've been pushing for the team to look at new innovations to speed recovery times for injured players."

The older man glanced down the hall where Tricia was making a rapid escape. "Dr. Reed. If you've got a minute, I'd like to talk to you about this research of yours."

Seeing her stop on a dime and turn, a look of complete surprise on her face, Royce had to force his expression to remain neutral when what he wanted to do was smile.

"Why would you want to do that?" she asked.

"I've been in this business my entire adult life. If there's one thing I've learned, it's if we don't change with the times, the times will change without us. There's a lot of stuff we take for granted today that didn't exist when I first started out. I'd be a fool to think everything that's ever going to be invented already exists."

"Don't you want to wait and see what happens with Mr. Ramirez?"

Herschel shrugged. "Does it matter what happens? Like Strikeout said, your program might not help him, but that doesn't mean it won't help the next guy who gets injured."

"I don't have much data yet. Not on the Mustangs, anyway. But I have the research I did with college athletes."

"You must have seen something positive in those results or you wouldn't be here now."

"You're correct…. I'm sorry, I didn't get your name."

"Herschel Ford, at your service." He extended his hand. After they shook hands, they headed down the hall toward Tricia's office, talking as they went.

Royce rubbed the back of his neck and watched them until they turned a corner. He hoped his efforts were received in the spirit he'd offered them. He really did believe in Tricia's work, even if no one would ever know exactly how she'd helped him. Because she had, he believed her work needed to continue. One way or the other, they'd find a way to make sure it was only used for the right purposes.

CHAPTER NINETEEN

Tricia stared into the freezer. Neither one of the two frozen dinners staring back at her held any appeal. As she closed the door and opened the one below to peer at the meager contents of her refrigerator, she faced the facts. She wasn't hungry. Reason stated she had to eat. It was going on 8:00 p.m., and she hadn't eaten anything since nibbling at the breakfast Clare Ramirez had fixed for them in the wee hours of the morning.

She'd spent the better part of the afternoon explaining her research and the data she'd collected to Mr. Ford. He'd seemed interested, and they had an appointment to talk again soon. Talking with the older man, she hadn't had time to worry about Tony, but alone in her apartment, she couldn't think about anything else. The more time that passed without word about how his session with the chiropractor had gone, the more her spirits dimmed. Since no one had called her she assumed her solution hadn't worked and he was still in pain. Most likely, they were prepping him for surgery already.

She'd purposely avoided thinking about Royce. He'd not

only been her first test subject, but he'd been sent to spy on her, too. She knew there were plenty of people who were suspicious of her intentions, but she'd never thought anyone would stoop to espionage. All they'd needed to do was ask and she would have answered all their questions. Instead, they'd sent a mole in to get the goods on her.

She'd been nothing but honest with him, and the League, but neither one had given her the same courtesy.

Royce had come to her defense today, telling everyone to give her a chance. They had nothing to lose by going with her recommendation. They were just being pigheaded and chauvinistic. No woman was going to infiltrate their good ole boys club and start telling them how to do their jobs. Not even if it meant saving one of their star players from undergoing a surgery he might not need. Thank God Royce had spoken up when he did.

When the doorbell rang, she jerked her head out of the refrigerator. Her heart stuttered, and her feet felt like lead weights anchoring her to the floor. Judging by the way they continued to push the button, whoever was at her door wasn't going away. Half the tenants of the apartment building were most likely plotting a murder right now. The walls were that thin.

Forcing her feet to move, she went to the door and looked through the peep hole. Royce Stryker stared back at her.

"Tricia. Open up. I know you're in there."

She was torn between never wanting to see the man again and wondering why he was there. If he had something to say to her, a phone call would have sufficed. He pressed the bell again. She rolled her eyes at the audacity of the man, and opened the door.

"Stop it! You're annoying my neighbors."

He didn't wait for an invitation. He advanced on her, and she instinctively backed away from the door. His gaze raked over the room behind her. "What took you so long? Do you have company?"

Tricia turned sideways, sweeping her arm to encompass

her tiny apartment. "As you can see, it's just me. Say what you've got to say, and leave."

"You're still mad at me."

"You bet your ass, I am." Tears she'd held at bay all afternoon threatened. "I was trying to help you, and you were there to spy on me."

"I'm sorry, sweetheart. I hated lying to you. If it's any consolation, I was just waiting for a time to meet with Doyle, so I could tell him he didn't have anything to worry about."

"I don't understand what he thought I was doing? I've explained my project to people at every level in the League."

"He had his concerns." He went on to explain the manager's worries about misuse of her research.

"That's absurd."

"Agreed, but I won't fault him for watching out for the players. Someone has to. Which brings me to why I'm here." He held up a dark bottle she hadn't noticed him carrying. "Champagne, compliments of Doyle Walker and the entire Mustangs Baseball organization." He headed for the kitchen, again without invitation.

"What are we celebrating?" It was obvious he wasn't going to leave, so she decided to go along for the time being. Champagne on an empty stomach probably wasn't a good idea, but she was beyond caring at this point.

"Tony's complete recovery, of course." He opened a cabinet door, shut it, and moved to another. "Where are your Champagne glasses?"

"I don't have any. Water glasses are to the right of the sink." She tried to tamp down the elation building inside her. For all she knew, they might have operated on the man today. "The surgery was a success?"

He set two glasses on the counter and slammed the cabinet door. Her neighbors were going to love her.

"He didn't have surgery." Royce went to work on the wire cage securing the cork. "It took some manipulating on the part of the chiropractor, but Tony's good as new. He's going to sit out tomorrow, give him some time to work the soreness out, but everyone agrees, he's good to go."

"Everyone?"

"Yeah." He thumbed the cork loose and poured a generous amount in each glass. "They X-rayed him enough to give him cancer or something, but couldn't find a thing wrong with him. He even took a few swings, and threw the ball a couple of times in the batting cage. Said he was a little stiff, but other than a little minor discomfort, he felt fine. He said to tell you you're his hero and the next bottle of bubbly is on him."

She took the glass he held out to her, lifting it to mirror the one he held aloft. "To you, Dr. Reed. You may have single-handedly saved the Mustangs' season." They clinked glasses.

Tricia let the bubbles dance on her tongue before she swallowed. She wasn't an expert on such things, but there wasn't anything cheap about the taste of the sparkling wine. She took another drink. "I didn't do anything."

"One of the things I love about you, Dr. Reed, is the fact that you aren't stupid. However, your last comment was one of the stupidest things I've ever heard."

Tricia placed the glass carefully on the counter. Drinking on an empty stomach had, indeed, been a bad idea. She could have sworn she just heard him say he loved her. "Not stupid if it's true."

His eyes narrowed to slits. He placed his drink next to hers. "Saying ridiculous things could get you spanked, Dr. Reed."

The thimbleful of alcohol she'd consumed, and hearing him say he loved her, made her reckless. She still wasn't sure why he was here. "Did you spank her, too?"

Wide-eyed, he asked, "Who? What the hell are you talking about?"

"The woman you left the stadium with the other night. Did you buy her expensive champagne and spank her?"

He shook his head as if to clear away an invisible fog then he focused his gaze on her. His face was tight, his lips a thin slash. "*That's* why you left?"

She nodded, no longer certain she'd done the right thing

bringing up his groupie. "There wasn't any reason for me to stay around. You had your game back. I'm sure you had your pick of partners for the evening."

Royce picked up his glass and drained it in one gulp. The pricey wine tasted bitter on his tongue. He'd known there had to be another reason Tricia left before he'd met up with her in Seattle—he'd just never dreamed it was because of Hannah. He knew he only had once chance to get this right. He chose his words carefully.

"The only person I wanted to share my success with was you. I rushed through interviews so I could get dressed and find you. Hannah, my ex-wife, was waiting for me in the players' lounge."

Tricia stiffened at the mention of his ex.

"I didn't know she was at the game. Hell, I don't know if she even was at the game. She might have shown up at the end, for all I know. She never mentioned my pitching, so if I had my guess, I'd say she didn't see the game." That would have been just like her, he thought. He couldn't remember the last time she'd paid any attention to his career.

"Anyway, when I first saw her, I thought she was there to deliver bad news. Maybe something had happened to someone in my family. Any one of them would have called her and sent her to tell me. As it turned out, she was there to try to get me to take her back. I refused. The last time I saw her, she was driving away from the restaurant where we had gone to talk."

Tricia seemed fixated on the two glasses sitting on the counter between them. He waited for her to say something, ask him anything. When she remained silent, he continued. "Sitting in the car outside the restaurant, I realized something I should have known long ago. I don't love Hannah. I haven't in a long time. We were high school sweethearts, Tricia. Sometimes love grows up with you, but for us, it didn't, though we both pretended it had. On my part, staying with her was comfortable. Having a wife insulated me from the Annies— women who hang out, hoping to lasso a professional ball player. I've never been one to hook up with that kind, and I never will be.

"I can only speculate about Hannah's reasons for staying as long as she did, but if I had to guess, I'd say it was the money. We didn't have much for a lot of years, but we both knew it was only a matter of time before I made it to the Majors and a big contract. Our marriage really began to crumble then. When she asked for a divorce, I was too busy with my career to look closely at what had gone wrong. I blamed myself for her unhappiness. The other night, I realized she had been happy to take the settlement I'd offered. She didn't really want me, she just wanted the money. She wanted to get back together with me because she's spent everything I gave her."

"You must not have given her very much. You've only been divorced, what, a year?"

"I'm going to spank you for that remark."

She jerked her head up. Heat rose to color her cheeks.

"You know me better than to believe I'd do something so cruel. I was more than fair with her."

"You don't play fair, Royce."

"You know that isn't true." It was time to throw his best pitch. She was ready for it, he could see the anticipation, the want and need in her eyes. "Maybe I haven't always played fair with you, but things are going to change. That's why I'm going to tell you this now. I want you to understand when I turn you over my knee and spank your impertinent ass, I'm doing it because I love you."

Fire sparked in her eyes.

"I love you, Tricia. Not because you gave me my game back, but because you are a remarkable woman. You're brave and fearless. You have a mind like a computer and a heart of gold. I love all of those things, but most of all, I love the way you trust me." He waited for the impact of his words to sink in before he extended his hand across the bar, palm up, silently asking her to demonstrate her trust.

Emotions bounced around inside her so fast it was nearly

impossible to grab hold of any one and make sense of it.

I love you. Oh, how those three little words twisted her world on its axis. In her wildest dreams—and she'd had some pretty wild ones since meeting Royce Stryker—she'd never imagined she'd hear him say those words to her. She hadn't even allowed herself to hope. Now, she wasn't sure she could trust her ears. But he was right about one thing, she trusted him with her body. It was her heart she worried about. Could she trust him with that as well?

The same unwavering gaze he employed on the mound held her under his spell. She trembled from head to toe, while his hand remained steady. Solid. Her body knew and craved his touch.

"Come with me. Trust me, Tricia. I'll never let you down."

Her body led the way, and her heart followed. She put her hand in his, accepting his reassurance, his promise, his love.

His fingers closed over hers, sealing the bond between them and sending a flood of warmth and certainty through her bloodstream. Her gaze dropped to their clasped hands. His, callused and strong, engulfed hers. A shiver raced down her spine.

"I'll never do anything to intentionally harm you."

Realizing he must have felt her body's reaction and misunderstood, she glanced up at him. "I know. I'm not afraid."

His expression told her he still didn't understand. For a man who made his living reading other people, he could be dense as a post. "I was thinking of how wonderful your hand was going to feel on my bottom."

A smile softened his features. "Were you now?"

"Yes."

His thumbs swept across her knuckles. "I wouldn't want to disappoint you." Without releasing her hand, he came around the bar and pulled her across the room.

As she watched him get comfortable on her sofa, anticipation dampened the folds between her legs. His strength and confidence overwhelmed her senses, yet she knew all the way down to her bones he'd never lift a hand to her in anger.

He pulled her down over his lap, taking every precaution to make sure she was as comfortable as possible. Angled so her torso rested on the cushion beside him, her toes barely made contact with the floor. Fully clothed, she felt exposed, yet safe.

He stroked her bottom with lazy circles, driving her crazy as she anticipated his first loving swat. "Tell me why you're going to get this spanking."

"Because I was disrespectful?"

"You questioned my honor, sweetheart. I've been less than honest with you these past weeks, but I've never given you any reason to believe I would treat Hannah unfairly, have I?"

"No." He hadn't. She'd said those things out of anger and frustration.

"No, what?"

"No, sir."

"For your lack of faith in me, I'm going to spank your bottom. Do you understand why I'm doing this?"

She nodded. Tears spilled from her eyes, creating a dark circle on her upholstery. The way he was gently caressing her backside while they talked only added to her remorse. How could he be so tender when she'd done her best to wound him? She sniffed back a sob. "Yes, sir. I'm sorry, sir. I knew what I said was wrong. I spoke in anger."

"I don't want you ever to think you can't speak your mind, but I won't have you throwing verbal darts at me for things I haven't done."

"I won't do it again. I promise."

The first blow landed with a *whump*, startling a gasp from her lips. Before she recovered from the first hard smack, he spanked her several more times. Her clothing insulated her from the sting, but did nothing to lessen the impact. She grabbed for a throw pillow and dug her fingers into it to keep from reaching back to shield herself from what she knew was to come.

As he massaged and rubbed her through the layers of

fabric covering her, she willed her body to relax. This was Royce. Every touch soft or stinging was given because she allowed it—craved it.

"Time to get down to business." His roughly spoken words were all the warning she received before his fingers slid beneath her waistband, dragging her running shorts and panties over her bottom. He didn't pull them all the way off, just took them far enough to expose her globes to his gaze.

Anticipation and blinding-hot desire stole the breath from her lungs. Was her bottom already red? Imagining his gaze admiring his handiwork had her squirming in his lap, begging for more.

"Be still." He clamped a hand on her left cheek and squeezed it hard enough to make her yelp. "If it gets too much for you, just say my name. I'll stop."

He placed a staying hand between her shoulder blades. Warmth radiated throughout her body, infusing her with a sense of safety. She felt a *swoosh* of cool air across her buttocks followed by the sharp bite of pain where his hand landed on her right cheek then again on her left. He peppered her backside with stinging slaps. She tried to count them in her head, but her usually agile mind couldn't keep up. After a while, he stopped and rubbed the sore places he'd created.

"Those were for putting your hands on Tony this morning. I fucking hate seeing you touch another man, even if it is your job."

His possessive jealousy brought a smile to her lips. She'd felt the same way about him when she saw him with the woman she now knew was his ex-wife. Her feelings at the time had cut deep, thinking if the tables were turned, he wouldn't experience the same betrayal. Already sliding down the slippery slope of love with the man, she didn't even try to save herself. She let go of the raveling rope end she'd been clinging to, and faster than a log in a water chute, she plummeted feetfirst into the murky waters of hopelessly in love.

Royce palmed her ass. Her soft skin was hot enough to

melt chocolate where he'd spanked her. But he wasn't through with her yet. She'd cut him to the core earlier with her remark about him not playing fair with his ex. Up until he'd spoken with Hannah the other night, he might have agreed with Tricia, but time, distance, and the woman's not-so-subtle plea for him to take her back had given him a new perspective. Not only had he been fair, he'd been generous to a fault. He hadn't told anyone, but part of the reason he hadn't bought furniture for his house was because he needed to accumulate some expendable cash. The amount he'd settled on Hannah had depleted his savings, leaving him enough to put a down payment on the house, but not enough to furnish it.

His financial situation was much better now. He'd even paid off the mortgage he'd initially taken out to purchase his home, putting off the furniture buying even longer. Maybe not the best move, but one he'd needed to take for himself. His shelf life as a professional athlete was short. Investing in real estate made more sense than investing in chairs and tables. And, he'd had no one to furnish the place for.

He massaged Tricia's sweet bottom and marveled at the way she'd changed his life. From the first moment he'd laid eyes on her, he'd known deep inside she wasn't going to be a casual acquaintance. He'd wanted her then, and he wanted her now. He would want her until the day he died, and then some, if the gods were kind to him.

His deep rose and scarlet handprints on her ass screamed, "Mine!" Possessing her had become an ache in his chest, and marking her as his, a need he no longer tried to deny. She was his. Always would be, and he planned on reminding her on a daily basis. But, for now, he needed her to understand how much her words had stung. Without warning, he brought his hand down on the rounded flesh of her right cheek. The slap sounded like the crack of a whip in the quiet room.

Tricia jerked and cried out. He spanked her just as hard on the other side. "This is fair, sweetheart." He continued to rein terror on her ass while she wiggled, jerked, and cursed him between sobs. He knew how she felt. He'd experienced the same level of pain when she'd made her accusation. The only difference was, she would carry the visible evidence of the pain, at least for a time, while his scars were all on the inside.

He half expected her to scream his name to get him to stop, but when the motion of his hand carried her scent up to his nostrils, he realized she'd gone beyond punishment. She was turned on by his spanking her, just as she had been the first time. And Lord knew he'd been hard for her since she opened the door wearing running shorts and a tank top.

Staying his hand in midair, he inhaled deeply. She'd thrown him a curve ball, making him need her like a crazy drunk needed another drink. He didn't know if he should swing or let the moment pass. He wanted a relationship with her, but they hadn't talked about anything more than him taking her over his knee. If he swung, slid her off his lap, and mounted her, would she call him out on a strike? Or would she run the bases with him?

The color on her ass was like a beacon, calling him. He'd punished her for lashing out at him in anger and made his point in regard to whom she belonged. The evidence was there in the shades of red painting her skin. *Mine.*

Covering her left cheek with his palm, he savored the lush curves on display. His cock ached to slip into her cleft, to stroke and tease the doors of her desire. He took his time, caressing her flesh, growing more desperate with every sigh, every moan, every twitch of her hips as he massaged the hurt away. He was damn lucky she'd let him touch her at all. He wasn't about to push his luck by taking more than she offered.

"Call me a pervert, but seeing my handprints on your ass turns me on like nothing else ever has."

A throw pillow she'd dragged beneath her chest muffled her response, but it sounded something like, *oh God,* to him. He wasn't sure if the exclamation was a good thing or a bad one.

He took a chance and slid his middle finger into the crease of her buttocks. She went completely still as he skimmed over the tight rosette, relaxing when he delved lower. His finger slid easily across her pussy, aided by her natural juices. He played with her folds then dipped inside her up to his first knuckle.

"Christ, Tricia. You're so hot and wet. I can't do this anymore. Seeing my handprints on your ass, feeling your body primed for fucking…. It's more than I can stand." He withdrew from her in one quick move, bringing more of her scent to his nose. He knew better than to lick her essence from his fingers. In the state he was in, tasting her would strain his control, possibly past its limits. Frantic, he looked for something to wipe his hand on. Spying a tissue box on the end table, he reached over Tricia's head. Before he could snag one, her slim fingers wrapped around his wrist.

"Don't." Hanging onto his arm, she wiggled off his lap to a kneeling position between his knees. She took his hand in both of hers, spread his fingers wide, and slowly, beginning with his thumb, took each one into her mouth.

When she got to his middle finger, he forgot how to breathe. Unable, or maybe just unwilling to stop her, he watched as she swept her tongue from base to tip—up one side then another before she sucked the digit into her mouth.

"Holy fuck!" He yanked his hand back before her ministrations sent him over the edge. He'd never come in his pants—not even when he was a randy teenager and the sight of a pair of tits had been reason enough to explode. He'd always prided himself on having more control. But Tricia had him riding the thin edge of restraint and loving every minute of it. "I need you. Now."

A saucy grin spread across her face. The little minx. She knew exactly what she was doing to him. He smiled back at her. "Don't think you're going to get away with teasing me, sweetheart. You'll pay for your actions later." He stretched one leg out, connected with the coffee table and shoved it back a foot. "Turn around. Brace yourself on the table."

While she situated herself, Royce stood, unfastening his pants. He pushed them down then worked one leg completely free. Good enough. Going down on one knee behind her, he gripped her hips. "Fuck." He stared at her reddened bottom and her pink pussy trapped between her legs held together by her shorts still wrapped tight around her thighs. A hidden treasure. If he didn't seize control of himself, he would fuck her to oblivion and back. *Breathe, fucker, breathe.*

He filled his lungs, belatedly realizing his mistake. Her scent went straight to his bloodstream like an alcohol drip. His head swam as blood rushed to his dick. Grabbing his throbbing appendage to stop himself from impaling her like a crazed animal, he stopped cold when his hand met with flesh.

"Shit. Fuck. Goddamnit!" He fumbled with his pants, found his wallet, and retrieved his emergency condom.

"What is it?"

"Hang on, sweetheart." *If this isn't a three-alarm emergency, I don't know what is.* He'd come within a second of fucking her bareback. God, he wanted to feel her, skin to skin, but until they talked about it, he wasn't taking any chances.

His mind flashed back to the family he'd seen in the stands the day Jason gave him the sage advice to get laid. He wanted that. The kids. The day at the ballpark. Only, he wanted to show his kids the game from field level. Wanted them to see how much their old man loved the game, and them.

As he positioned his cock at the wet opening of her pussy, another image flashed across his consciousness. Tricia—round with his child. The fantasy was gone as fast as it came, but he knew he would move heaven and earth to make it a reality. Holding her hips firm in his grasp, he drove his cock deep. Blind with pleasure, he paused to catch his breath and savor the feel of her tight, wet channel surrounding him. Her warmed bottom was a soft cradle for his hips.

"Okay, sweetheart?"

"God, Royce. Move. Please."

The pleading tone in her voice mirrored his own need. "This is going to be quick." He pulled out so only the head of his cock was inside her. "We'll do it slow, later."

"Just do it. Please."

Knowing she was onboard with the urgency of their situation released the grip he had on his control. He slammed into her, burying his cock balls deep, rocking her so hard the coffee table slid out from under her. She was on all fours, just the way he wanted her. When he pulled back, she pushed her hips toward him, begging him to fill her again. It was an invitation he couldn't refuse.

The rhythm he set was fast-paced, but she stayed with him, rocking her ass to take more of him. Nothing short of a nuclear explosion would have stopped him from taking her, claiming her as his. His balls were drawn up so tight he wasn't sure he'd ever see them again, but he was determined to make this one good for her, too. He couldn't promise her a drawn-out affair, but he could try to take her along with him when he came.

Reaching between them, he located his cock sliding slick and wet in and out of her pussy. From there, it was easy to find her pubic bone and apply pressure. From the sounds coming from her throat, he was pretty certain he had found the spot he'd been searching for. He matched the pressure from his fingers with his cock, shoving deep inside her. It only took a few thrusts before her body tensed.

"Royce!"

Her pussy contracted around him, the hot, wet flood of her orgasm enveloping him.

"God, sweetheart. You feel so fuckin' good." Powering into her, he sought his own release. When it came, the pleasure bordered on pain.

Gripping her around the waist, he sat back on his heels, bringing her with him so she sat on his thighs. He hooked his chin over her shoulder and pressed his temple to her cheek. They rode out the aftershocks locked together.

He didn't want to let go of her, but his legs started to cramp. How catchers squatted for as long as they did, he had no idea. "I've got to stand up," he said, easing the tight grip he had on Tricia's waist. Her sigh said everything he was thinking. "I know. I don't want to move either, but if I don't, I won't be able to tomorrow and I have to pitch."

She crawled off him only to roll to her back on the floor,

arms outstretched, her eyes closed. His mouth watered at the sight. Her tank top was hitched up around her waist, leaving her bare down to where her shorts hugged the top of her thighs. Her disheveled appearance and the glow of satisfaction on her face depicted a woman who'd been well and truly fucked. He committed the image to memory, knowing he would remember this moment for the rest of his life.

He sat on the edge of the sofa, pulled his other pant leg off then his shirt before heading to the bathroom to dispose of the condom. Tricia was right where he'd left her when he returned. He crouched beside her, and though he hated to mess with her picture-perfect pose, he wanted her naked. When he tugged on her shorts, she smiled and straightened her legs, passively aiding him toward his goal.

"Up you go," he said as he slid an arm beneath her shoulders and lifted.

She was as limp as a noodle, but she managed to raise her arms so he could remove her top. Her bare breasts popped free of the built-in-bra thingy. Bracing her upright with one arm, he leaned in for a taste. In the first real sign of life in her since he'd pushed her off his lap, she wrapped her arm around his head, cradling him to her breast.

Royce amused himself, moving from one breast to the other until her nipples were hard little nubs. Moaning, she stroked her needy mound herself.

"How about we finish this in bed?" With a little help from her, he lifted her into his arms and carried her into the bedroom. He placed her on the bed then stretched out beside her. His cock was ready for action, but he was determined to take it slow this time. To be on the safe side, he rolled on a fresh condom. The last thing he wanted to do was call a time-out in the middle of the inning.

He palmed one of her breasts, and she arched her back. He brushed his thumb over her nipple, chuckling as it puckered to a hard point.

She snaked a hand between them. He stopped her before she reached her destination. Guiding her hand up, he pressed it against the mattress above her head.

"Strikeout?"

"What, sweetheart?" He switched his attention to her other breast, lavishing it with attention.

"You aren't playing fair."

He couldn't help but chuckle. "Do you want me to last long enough to satisfy you?"

"God, yes."

He loved her throaty reply. "Then keep your hands to yourself, sweetheart."

"Royce?"

He released her breast then tongued her puckered nipple. "Hmm?"

"Stay with me?"

Using a knee to spread her legs, he settled himself above her. The tip of his cock burrowed inside her. He wasn't going anywhere. "Forever, sweetheart. Forever."

ABOUT THE AUTHOR

USA Today Best-Selling author Roz Lee is the author of over thirty romances. The first, The Lust Boat, was born of an idea acquired while on a Caribbean cruise with her family, and soon blossomed into a five-book series originally published by Red Sage. Following her love of baseball, Roz turned her attention to sexy athletes in tight pants, writing the critically acclaimed Mustangs Baseball series.

Roz has been married to her best friend, and high school sweetheart, for over four decades. They have two daughters and are the proud grandparents of three adorable grandkids. Roz and her husband live in the wilds of New Jersey with their Labrador Retriever, Bud which is code for Big Unruly Dog.

Even though Roz has lived on both coasts, her heart lies in between, in Texas. A Texan by birth, she can trace her family back to the Republic of Texas. With roots that deep, she says, "You can't ever really leave."

When Roz isn't writing, she's reading or traipsing around the country on one adventure or another. No trip is too small, no tourist trap too cheesy, and no road unworthy of travel.

www.RozLee.net